Also by Wanda D. Hudson:

Wait for Love: A Black Girl's Story

LuvMe

Miss Luv's Books

www.wandadhudson.com

I0517507

Cover Design: CANDACEK –
www.cckwebdev.com

ACKNOWLEDGEMENTS

I thank God for making me ME. For continuing to guide and bless me with gifts that He knew would make my life wonderful. Thank you.

To my family, friends and supporters, I thank you for continuing to spread the word about Miss Luv's Books.

I luv you.

Wanda D. Hudson

DATING
WANDA

®Miss Luv's Books

Because Everybody Needs A Little Luv!

Forget about kissing a few frogs. He will send you the man for you.

~Wanda D. Hudson

∞ *Bubble Intuition* ∞

The problem with being single is that everyone who isn't single has a problem with your non-existent love life. Single women always receive disappointing comments disguised in the form of concern.

"You shouldn't be alone."

"I don't know why no one has snatched you up."

"If I wasn't married I'd make you my woman."

For the record, if you weren't married your dumbass would be single and one step from the grave. Are these sympathy lines? Are they said to get easy panty access? The ones that come from women are the worst.

"I'm so glad I'm married and don't have to deal with dating."

The word bitch runs through my mind silently as my response. Does being single equate to being pitiful? And why is it when you meet someone you're interested in they have a problem with that? Pity comments change to protective ones.

"Oh, you better watch him. He looks sneaky."

"Does he have kids? You don't need no baby mama drama."

"You were better off when you were single."

Should I be confused or should the person who is asking the question be? I don't know why we say the things we do; blame it on the world we live in, I guess. What I do know is that if one more person asks me why I don't have a man I'm going to go Ms. Pacman on them. Chewing folks up and shoving a joystick down their throat when I'm done.

Before we continue, I have to set the record straight. I'm not desperate, begging or looking. I have had a few men folk in my time. Being single is okay with me. Would I like a husband? Sure. We weren't placed on this earth to live alone. One thing I've learned is being single is much better for my life than being with Captain Crazy who got cut from the Super Friends and can't save a damn thing – especially money.

My high profile dating life can be compared to a clearance sale box of Valentine's Day chocolate. I'd take a bite out of an unknown morsel and sometimes get a piece of good shit. A few times it was some sort of what the fuck deal. Mostly it was the okay kind, you know, you really don't like it – but not enough to not deal with it.

Everyone has a story to tell and get ready because I'm going to tell you a few of mine. Broke, busted, black and angry. Hmmm, that could be the title of one of my tales. To protect me, these tales are fictitious with a twist of luv. If you happen to see yourself in one, well, uh, don't tell anybody.

We all have a friend or know someone who has the nosiest female in their circle. I know one and her name is Pat. If she didn't greet me every time I see her with the same tired hello, I'd think she wasn't breathing.

"Wanda P. Hilson! *How you doin'*?" (Wendy Williams and Madea have corrupted a lot of people.) Girl, I'm blessed and highly favored and walking in the Spirit of the Holy Ghost! You got a man yet?"

"Why are you so loud, and why do you always call me by my full name?"

"You oughta be glad! It ain't like a man is calling your name!"

I should stab her.

"Hey, Pat."

"I asked you did you have a man yet? I guess not since you lookin' all dry this mornin'!"

You can tell when a woman has gotten her back dug out. Her mouth is real flip and she takes shit talking to the level of getting slapped as a response in 5 seconds or less.

"If my personal life was any of your business I'd answer the question."

"You just did! Girl, you need to at least get you some. How long has it been now anyway?"

Yes, her back has another groove in it. I guess her husband hit it from behind because that helium balloon belly of his stops all front activity. His fatass is too heavy to float away, though. Picture a whale humping a beach ball. That is so wrong of me. I hope I'm not secretly jealous.

"Wanda stop daydreaming. How long has it been?"

"Why do you need to know that? You're mighty perky. Did you have a good night?"

"Hell yeah!"

Pat and Jeremy have been married for six years. They're both round as hell and all I can picture is a walrus/sea lion type combo. Slimy fat shit that just can't connect. Loneliness will make you do some strange things, like pretend bad dick is better than aight'.

"Jeremy came home with two forties and it was on after that!"

"He's fifty-two and still drinking forties? Damn...."

"Well, at least I got somebody to drink and have sex with!"

"Pat, it's not all about just having somebody. It's more to it than that for me."

"Yea, whateva...that's what all you horny chicks say!"

Once again I want to stab her. This time I'm aiming for her throat. Why is she laughing like that? All doubled over and shit. I don't think what she said was that funny.

"What do you want, Pat? Don't you have a meeting to go to or lunch or something?"

"Alright, alright, I'm sorry. I came over here to ask you if you'd like to go out on a date with Jeremy's brother's friend. He has a good job at the bread store. Shoot, he hooks us up with day old bread all the time."

Pat's neck was swaying and her lips were smacking and flapping. Fat ass.

"No, I'm not interested."

"Why not? You at least have to try to meet people. You're gonna be single till you die!"

"I've met some of Jeremy's friends. Day old bread and a forty is not my idea of a date."

"Oh, so you picky now?"

Eye rolling and sucking her teeth were bad enough. She had her hands on her wide ass hips, which meant I would have to battle my way out of this one.

"He's really attractive and a nice guy."

"So why doesn't he have somebody if he's such a good catch?"

"He was engaged and the woman called it off."

"Why?"

A long hot sigh escaped her before she answered.

"Well, he just wasn't ready to get married yet."

"How long were they engaged?"

"Twenty years...but that doesn't mean he'll never get married. They just weren't meant for each other."

"Pat, get outta here with that. Twenty years? That's ridiculous!"

"Okay, wait a minute; just wait a minute before you let a great guy get away. Jeremy sent me a picture of him. Just look at it before you give me a final no."

I watched as she fumbled with her cell trying to locate the picture. Why she was so eager to get me a man was annoying, but kind of cute, too.

"Here he is! Look at him? Ain't he fine?"

Pat thrust her phone into my hands and the heavens opened up. Damn, he *was* fine. Dark brown, salt and pepper hair and a nice muscular build.

"*This* is Jeremy's friend? He must've sent you the wrong picture." All Jeremy's friends were round and greasy. Crisco greasy. A bunch of slimy shiny bastards.

"I told you he was fine. Just one dinner date? Please?"

A woman's intuition never fails her, but a fine man stomps it into ant crumb pieces every time. The butterflies in my stomach weren't there for the joy of a giddy little girl finding her knight in shining armor. No, this was a flutter of the bubble guts about to let loose. Some shit was about to happen.

That workday ended with me agreeing to go on one dinner date with Lenword. Lenword? What the hell? Lenword Alvin Crumpter was the manager of Day Old Gold, a store that received daily deliveries from local bakeries of expired breads and such. They were resold for half the price or donated to soup kitchens. He'd worked there for over 20 years, having started out as a driver, then a short stint as a cashier before becoming the top dog.

My first question is why do people pretend to be what they're not? My second is do they even think about what will happen when their cover is blown? You can't keep crazy silent forever; it comes out at some point. I mean, it's crazy, and that's what crazy does.

Pat shoved his number down my throat and I called him that night. Is it a mistake for a woman to call a man? Some men yes. Their ego gets the best of them and then their over active imagination begins spinning out of control.

While I waited to leave a message I was treated to a Lenny Williams song. I laughed when I heard it and thought *thank God for different musical tastes*.

"I'm a grown man...doing what grown mens do...I can't help it girl...I like dat hoochie coochie cooooo."

"Hello, Lenword, this is Wanda, Pat's friend. Please give me a call when you have a chance. My number is..."

"Wanda? Wanda? Hey! This is LAC! Hey gurl!"

What the hell? Why is he yelling?

"Oh, hey. Uh, yea..." The yelling gave me an instant attitude.

"Yeah, gurl! Pat told me you'd probably call. I was weight lifting and was in the middle of a set. I gotta keep my body right!"

Instant turnoff. Why? The loud voice and the sly bragging were annoying. Bread baking bastard.

"Well, exercise is good. If this is a bad time...."

"Do you exercise?"

Did his dumbass just cut me off? "Excuse me?"

"Oh, oh, oh, oh...I'm sorry. I didn't get to see a picture of you. I was trying to get a visual. Hehehehehehe."

Suddenly I was transported to the nineteen seventies. Pimps up hos down became my silent mantra.

"I'm sorry...I'm sorry. Let's start over. Hello?"

Hmmm, an excellent attempt to clean up a potential mess. I don't have anything to lose.

"Hi, may I speak to Lenword?"

"This is Lenword. And who may I ask is the beholder of the beautiful voice on my line?"

Go, pimp, go.

"This is Wanda. I got your number from Pat. You can call me back if this isn't a good time."

Giving him the option of calling me back makes me seem less anxious and gives him control.

"Naw, naw. Pat told me you might call. I'm going to get straight to the point. I don't care for talking on the phone. How about you meet me tomorrow night for dinner? Your choice, my treat."

Wow! Pimpin' is easy and unfortunately, so am I.

"Now that's a deal. How about 7PM at Nikki Tees? They have a large variety of dishes and the atmosphere is very nice. Have you ever been there before?"

"I've gotten food to go, but I've never sat inside and had a nice meal. Nikki Tees it is. I can't wait to meet you. You already know what I look like and I know you're fine. I can tell by your voice."

Why was I smiling? Because I was fine, and hearing a potential man that may be mine for the long haul sounded great.

"Thank you Lenword. See ya tomorrow."

Okay, the first mistake I made was agreeing to meet him so soon. Why was he so eager? I should've taken at least one lengthy phone conversation to investigate. Was he a serial killer? Pussy hound? Basement dweller? I guess I'll find out in between Chicken Florentine, and wait, since he's paying I'll have steak. If the date ends early at least I'll have a doggie bag that will make a pit bull proud.

Pat hounded me most of the next day with background details. Lenword was 56, never married and owned a four apartment building in the South Bronx. He lived in one of them and collected income from the rest. The Pillsbury Doughboy had nothing on him as she said. He had one sister who had five kids and was a great fill in father.

"Where is the children's father?"

"She's trying to get on Maury to find out."

I stared waiting for Pat to laugh and tell me the truth. She kept talking as if what she said was normal. Once again the bubble guts started to churn.

It would take me about thirty minutes to get to Nikki Tees from work. My outfit that day was black business suit dapper, and since I didn't want to look like I was being interviewed for a job I brought a change of clothes with me. A four inch pair of eggplant pumps along with a knee-length navy wrap dress wouldn't make me look thirsty, but single enough to be available.

Each time Pat walked by my office she smiled, and then pretended to have major activity on her phone. I thought it strange that she didn't hound me about my date that evening. Just when I began to think I was home free she made me imagine myself choking her until the grim reaper asked me to stop.

"Soooooooo, Miss Lonely, Tired and Horny, are you all set for your date tonight?"

Some bitches are real bitches. I mean, that's all they know how to be.

"And how was your night?"

"Why are you all up in my business?"

"Trouble in paradise?" Every time she was in a foul mood Jeremy was the cause of it. He might have stayed out all night. He probably received texts from another female "friend". Knowing him he stared at a woman's breasts. Or he could have been breathing to loud. One time he came to pick her up and we all rode the elevator together. I caught him staring a hole through a woman's blouse. He turned everything into a buffet. Fatass.

"Jeremy came home late last night. He said he fell asleep at his desk and nobody woke him up. People are always hatin' on us."

"Pat, Jeremy is the front desk security officer at the hospital. He's security; isn't he supposed to be up watching everybody else?"

"See, that's what I mean. More hate. So what he fell asleep? He works hard. Now he's suspended. People get on my nerves."

"Okaaaay."

"Anyway, are you all set for your date? What time are you meeting at Nikki Tees?"

"Who told you we were going there?" I can't stand a man who runs his mouth.

"Lenword called me last night and told me."

"Called you for what?"

"Oh, girl, calm down. He wanted my opinion on how you looked and I told him."

"What?"

"Don't worry about it. I hooked you way up! I said you and Jill Scott could be sisters except you're the ugly one."

There is a reason for workplace violence. Still flapping her mouth with no regard to her fucked up comment she continued.

"I told him you hadn't had a man in a long time so he was in for a good night."

Her vibrating cell saved her life.

"Girl I gotta go; this is Jeremy. Call me when you get home tonight – I wanna know all the details."

Even when you do have something to say, don't say anything. You'll save yourself a lot of grief.

I planned to work until 5:30. That would give me enough time to freshen up and go from Diana Prince to Wonder Woman. Lenword sent me two text messages that put a smile on my face. The first asked how I was doing. The second said he couldn't wait to meet me that evening. I responded in kind and half thought about sending a text exactly when I left work to say I was on my way. Thinking those were the things that couples do I stopped myself. Yes, it's courteous, but a cloud of desperation is hanging on, too.

Wednesday nights were the beginning of the weekend at Nikki Tees. The atmosphere was live and it instantly put me in a festive mood. 5'8", brown skin and 180lbs landed in all the right places. My wrap was fresh and my lips were eye catching - this sista here was ready. Pat was off with her Jill Scott comparison – there was definitely nothing ugly about me.

"Hi, welcome to, Nikki Tees. Table for one?"

"Hi. No, I'm meeting someone. I'm not sure if he's here yet."

"Oooooooh, is your name, Wanda?"

I quickly glanced at the hostess' nametag. Sabrina was working hard for her tip. A porn star movie smile formed on my lips. Damn. Desperation is not going to ruin this for me. Wait, am I desperate? Jesus...

"Yes it is."

"Good! Follow me!"

Sabrina took me midway through the restaurant before she began to zero in on one particular table. Lenword looked up from his phone and a huge grin met us. He stood as we approached.

"Here you go. I'll send a waitress right over."

Sabrina winked at me as she turned to leave. She must be single, too.

"Well, well, well, this is my lucky night. The pleasure is all mine."

Lenword reached his hand out and took mine into his. He raised it to his lips and planted a wet kiss on the inside of my wrist. That shit was nasty. Too much spit nasty. I'm damn sure not wiping it on my dress. I hope I don't need a tetanus shot. Here we go...

"You're much prettier than I thought. I was going to call and cancel. I'm glad I didn't."

He came around and pulled my seat out. That gave me a chance to look him up and down. A red dress shirt with a brown bow tie, grandpa

Wrangler jeans and dirty Adidas? What? No...this was a set up. The return of Candid Camera was happening tonight. I would not make them the top rated show and make a fool of myself. Not tonight. He did look like his picture, though. Depending on how he carried himself he either had lines of maturity on his face or hard life cracks. His hair was cut low and in spite of his no fashion sense he was neat.

"So, Wanda, how was your day?"

"It was good. I stay busy and it helps."

"Now what is it that you do?"

"I'm the Promotions Director at Bizzy Fiz Entertainment. We provide entertainment for various functions like -"

"Hold that thought, I wanna show you something."

Did this ass just interrupt me? He wasn't looking at me when I was talking, either. He placed a purse, oh excuse me, man bag on the table and had been rustling through it since we sat down.

A slick giggle ran from his mouth.

"Have you ever seen one of these?"

He giggled again and opened his hand to show me a small pink rubber pig that was attached to a key chain. My eyes went from his face to his hand a few times before I answered.

"No, what is it?"

Why he was startled when the waitress approached I'll probably never know. Quickly, he closed his hand tight and slid it off the table.

"May I take your drink orders?"

Lenword had a rushed look on his face. Whatever was in his hand was obviously more important than our drinks.

"Uh, I haven't decided yet. Can you give us a few more minutes?"

He made a loud *massa I'm free* sound. That's the only thing I can think of to equal his sound of relief. Either the pink pig held cocaine or diamonds, or he was a fool. Regardless of which one it was, I was ready to find out.

When the waitress was out of sight he slid his hand back onto the table and opened it. A crooked grin was on his face and he began to squeeze the pig and giggle. Each time he squeezed it a brown substance came out of its ass.

"Here, you try it." He waited for me to take the pig and kept giggling. I didn't remove it from his hand and opted to give it a quick squeeze and let it go.

"Uhm, what is so special about your keychain?"

"Isn't it amazing the way the shit slides in and out of the ass? That's funny!"

BINGO! I'm talking full card bingo, too. Now I get why the bubble guts showed up. Bubble intuition never fails. This fool is a straight up day old bread baking ass freak. And an aggressive one at that. Awww, hail naw. Our first date and you're dropping dirty anal sex hints right out the box? At least let me get a drink and a sandwich. Dusty bas'tid!

"Yea, I guess it is kinda funny." Dusty ass bas'tid... "Uh, when the waitress comes back can

26

you order a coke for me? I need to go to the ladies room."

"Sure, no problem! Do whatever you gotta do to get ready. We got all night!"

What the? "Uh, yea, I'll be right back."

Lenword definitely would not get a call back after this audition. 56? I should've thanked him for keeping it real. When you get older it makes no sense to waste time so I applaud him for that. As I made my way to the front door I turned to glance at him one more time. He was going hard with the pink pig. Squeezing it and touching the brown stuff as it came out. I think it was rubber cement. Next time I'll pay closer attention to my bubble intuition. When my guts get'ta rumbling some shit was sure to be close behind. Lenword...tsk, damn ass freak. I'll make sure I slap the shit out of Pat first thing in the morning.

∞ *Vegetarian Beans* ∞

Working in a promotions department affords me the opportunity to see various creative ideas. Some I love, others, well; I'll just say creativity speaks to whoever wants to listen. I meet a lot of different people and during one of my many conferences I met Parker.

How shall I describe Parker to you? Let's see... I'll give you the truth. Parker is a lying sorry broke ass that has an excuse for everything. Shit can't do shit for him.

When Parker and I met he said he'd been with Hot Spots Limousine Service for close to 2 years. I take a lot of the blame for wasting time with him. I should've asked more questions. He was a volunteer for 20 months and had only been employed for 2 of those months. Close to 2 years as an employee is incorrect. He also said he made $80,000 a year. Upon further investigation and I Spy questioning he said, "I never said that. I said I can make up to $80,000 a year if I work 3 full time jobs and a part time one." Asshole.

"Hey, girl. What'chu thinking about now? Are you all set for your meeting this afternoon?"

"Hey, Pat. Yes, I'm ready. Are you going to sit in on this one?"

"Hell no! Yah'll are boring. I'll be down the hall in the Media Room watching my soaps. If you need anything buzz me."

She walked off before I could respond. Ever since the Lenword thing she's backed off a bit. It's been 3 weeks since that happened so I know she's just waiting for the right time to get all up in my business again. Lenword told her he didn't find me attractive so he left. He's the definition of a dusty ass bas'tid for real.

Pat makes me think about things to the point where I analyze them to no end. I never thought of myself as lonely. Pat and Jeremy's relationship is two lonely people that can't stand being alone. Who wants to be somebody's something to do until? My foray into getting to know Parker was exactly that. He was something to do.

During the 2 month time frame that we had gotten to know each other one nagging fact that I felt about him wouldn't go away. Parker was some kind of pitiful ass. You know the type of person that can't fend for themselves or figure anything out. They stare into space and try to bond with their celestial leader. If it isn't laid out for them they don't know which way to go. It really bothered me because when he ran his mouth about promotional business people patted him on the back. On a personal level he was mentally revoked and reversed. His dumb ass mind traveled in backward motion. Parker can make you twist your face up and get a migraine afterwards.

My private intercom light began flashing signaling me to an outside call.

"Hello?"

"Uhmmmmmmm, hello?"

Oh here we go with the bullshit. "Hi, Parker. What's up?"

"Uhmmmmmm, I need a ride home. Can you come get me now?"

"No. I'm going into a meeting in 15 minutes."

"Well can't you come get me first? It won't take you that long."

He didn't drive and always called me, his personal taxi, asking for a ride. He was on a fairy tale magic carpet ride trip. Ain't shit funny about a grown man that can't drive nor give up gas money to get where he wants to go.

"How long is your meeting going to take? My back has been bothering me and if I have to take the subway I'll be in pain."

Not my fault, bitch "Parker, I said no. I'll give you a call later. Maybe we can grab something to eat."

"So you're not going to come? I gotta sit here and wait until you get off?"

"No, you can go home. I'll call you later."

"But I just told you about my back."

If you have to try to be nice to someone you're doing too much. Relationships should flow naturally. Most times when Parker was around I became aggravated and had to pretend that I actually liked him. Why bother? I guess I just wanted something to do. Never ignore the warning signs.

"If you asked me I'd come and get you."

People always say that when they know damn well that their "if" scenario will never be.

"I'm not coming to get you."

"Fine. Call me later."

He slammed the phone down which caused me to laugh. On my way home I'll stop by his place and end this. We hadn't had sex yet and never showed each other any form of affection. I think I was his fix it all and he was my, well, hmmm, yeah, he was my something to do.

Tennille, the Executive Assistant to the company President sashayed into my office.

"What's up, Miss Luv? Are you going to do comedy at the bosses 65th birthday party?

"Do you want me to get fired?"

Tennille's laugh was a cross between a cuddly teddy bear and a stuck pig. Sometimes it was cute, but most times irritating. She's my girl so I never told her to cut her vocal cords.

"Girl, they already know you have a mouth on you. I'm organizing it with his wife and can get you some good pay. Think about it, okay?"

"How about I host it instead? I can recommend some good comedians. It'll still be a good time."

"You know what? I'm going to run that by Mrs. Harris. She wanted to host it, but her ass is so dry. With you doing it she can mingle and get drunk like she always does.

Tennille and I both laughed. Over the summer the company held a mix and mingle affair and Mrs. Harris was more than the life of the party. Her old ass got to' up! She danced with a bikini top on and boy shorts. I will admit that she looks good for a 68 year old woman who has undergone extensive plastic surgery. Still, nasty don't play favorites. It loves everybody.

"So what are you doing this weekend? Tim wants to go to Dell's for wings and shoot pool. I'm tired of going there. They make ghetto drinks. The last time we went Shelly put gin, whiskey and scotch in a glass and called it a Long Island Iced Tea."

"You know Shelly isn't a bartender. She's dating the owner; you know how that goes."

"Are you still talking to Parker?"

"Funny you should ask. When I leave I'm going by his place and end it. Parker can't do shit for me."

Tennille laughed and then covered her mouth as if to say she was sorry.

"Girl, please. Let it out. He's always whining or complaining. Something about him just doesn't sit right with me. He always wants to use my things or have me drive him somewhere. I didn't give up the ass yet either. Just annoying."

"Good, cut him loose. There is someone who'll be at the meeting I think is perfect for you anyway."

"Tennille..."

"If you let Pat set you up you can let me."

Ouch. "That was cold...real cold."

"His name is Braxton Lewis and girl he is fine! He's the Digital Content Manager at Visual Demon. Single, no kids, educated and stable."

"Can I at least get past Parker?"

"Deal! See you in a bit."

Tennille left and I gathered my note pad and vision board for the meeting. Pat had set up the room and all I had to do was be me. We were working with a new client and they were hesitant on a few of our suggestions. I could sell Stevie Wonder a pair of colored contact lens so I really wasn't worried.

As I walked down the hall I thought my mind decided to become a losing lottery ticket. I'd bet money that I heard Parker's voice.

"I'll wait here for her. She's going to give me a ride home."

What the? That sorry bas'tid. My feet began to stomp down the hall and I wanted to hurdle over the desk and choke his crisp ass when I saw him.

"Parker what are you doing here?"

My nose flared like a bull on the attack.

"You said you'd give me a ride home, remember?"

His mama breastfed him with a dick.

"Parker? Just sit down...please, just sit down and I'll be out later."

I couldn't wait to leave work and blast his ass. I should just slap the shit out of him right now. Come to think about it I don't even find him attractive. Sometimes he looks decent and others he's just there. I can't be desperate; I just can't. Look at his stupid ass standing there licking his lips and looking at mine. If a dog were watching a hump fest it would look like Parker. Them shits are really chapped, too. How could I not see this?

His cell phone rang and he tried to look important by yelling into it. And then the dirty fingernails. Dirty nails don't equate to hard work, it means you need a good ass washing. Damn fool.

He put his caller on hold and asked a bitch ass question. What he said solidified me ending all contact with him throughout my next few lifetimes.

"Can you get me something to drink? I'll wait in your office because I need to use the computer."

"No...and just wait here."

Pat was smacking her gum and looked at me like her pot had boiled over. I know she couldn't wait to run and tell all of this.

Taking a few deep breaths calmed me as I walked into the meeting. I smiled as I scanned the room and walked to the front to begin the presentation. Everybody looked familiar except for two. I'd never seen the female before. She was quite flashy – purple hair, gigantic silver hoops flashy, so my guess was that she worked with the Video Production Team. The sexy cup of solid hot hazelnut without cream had to be Braxton Lewis. Tennille was on point with the fine comment. Midnight was my preference but after seeing all the swag that the President has ain't nothing wrong with afternoon activity, too.

"Hello. I'm Wanda and I'd like to thank you for coming to the *final* concept meeting."

Light snickers filled the room. We had met a few times before and hadn't settled on anything. Something as simple as a change in a layout color – black or purple, had stalled the go ahead. I was ready to put this baby into orbit thanks to Parker giving me extra gasoline to get things blazing.

Before I could ask his name Braxton made his formal introduction.

"Hello, Wanda. I'm Braxton Lewis. I work with the Digital Content team at Visual Demon. This is my assistant, Lacy. We're looking forward to finalizing this today and working closely with you."

"Hi, Braxton...Lacy. I'm sure this short video will meet all of your needs. Let's get started."

Braxton smiled before he reclaimed his seat. Horny will make a ho out of anybody. I had to work hard to focus on the sale and not him. Then I remembered Parker. The thought of dropping him and picking up something that could be long lasting made me get the job done.

"Well, that concludes this presentation. In keeping with the initial agreement we would like to receive all suggestions and changes within a 48 hour period. "

"That won't be necessary."

Braxton stood once again and held the room's attention.

"Please revise the contract to include this design and I'll have it signed and back to you this afternoon. I love it!"

Just when I was about to secure a lunch meeting with Braxton, Pat appeared.

"Excuse me. I'm sorry to interrupt, but can I see you for a minute, Wanda?"

The cock blocking fuck was at it again. On my way out of the room I stopped and made sure Braxton would meet me again.

"Braxton please excuse me. I have to run an errand. I'll give you a call tomorrow morning so we can set up a meeting, okay?"

"I'd love that. I'll talk to you soon."

We shook hands and he wrapped both of his around mine. Yeah, I can't wait to talk to him.

Hurrying back to my office I grabbed my purse and coat. You know how you get excited when you're going to buy something new or get money? I had that kind of blood pumping through my veins. That I'm about'ta fuck you up blood. When I reached the front of the office Parker was standing up.

"I've been waiting a long time."

I didn't bother to respond and instead held the door open for him to exit. A male bitch is the worst thing to deal with. I waited until we were seated in my car before I spoke.

"Parker, this isn't working out. I'll take you home today and once you get out don't call, email, or text me again. I don't like you. I feel like I'm the man and you're the woman. It's just not working."

Parker sighed and sucked his teeth. Bitch.

"You know, I wish you would re-think your decision. I have a special evening planned for us. I'm sorry if I got on your nerves; I was anxious to see you."

The remainder of the ride was in silence. It took 30 minutes to get to his place but it felt like 3 hours. I pulled up, put the car in park and waited for him to get his ass out.

"Please come in. Let me show you that I can be the man you want."

A begging man can be a turn on – a begging bitch? I should've kicked him out while the car was moving. The tuck and roll move has saved many lives.

"Parker, I said it was over."

"Please?"

I sighed and parked. Why? I have no idea. This time he held the door open for me. I was surprised to see that he actually lived in a decent house. Something must be up with this and I really didn't care. We went in and he didn't bother to put his things down or show me around. He went straight to a room that was too small to be a studio. I didn't ask but it looked more like he was renting a room within the house. There was shit piled on top of shit. I can't stand clutter or sloppy people. Uh-uh, Parker was definitely not the one.

"Can I get you something to drink?"

"Listen, I'm tired and I really don't want to be here. No I don't want anything to drink. What is it that you had planned?"

He gave me a grimy smile and turned on music. His musical system played 8 Track Tapes. Nothing wrong with nostalgia but the music sounded warped and slow. When he lowered his voice a few octaves I almost lost it.

"Do you like Barry White, Wanda?"

What the fuck? Then he really lost his little damn mind. He began taking off his clothes. Everything exploded. Stomach, ass, hips and thighs busted out like a broken box from a KFC variety meal. He had on a pair of black dress pants. A girdle or spanx had to be sewn in them somewhere. Shock held me for a minute. I hadn't seen a naked man in a while and I actually looked at his crotch. I wanted to see if he was packing. Not that I would unwrap it; I just wanted to know. I squinted, opened my eyes wide, and then squinted again. Parker's shit looked like a big ass clit.

A demonic sound came from him then.

"Do you like what you see?"

Suddenly everything fell into place. That something that I couldn't put my finger on. Look like a man but act like a beeeeyatch should've been the disclaimer on his birth certificate. His ass was confused.

"Wanda, I love you."

Bitch please did a quick tango with my tongue. I managed to dip it before it escaped. He tried to do a sexy head move. It looked more like a bobble head that was dying in slow motion instead. Dumbass.

"If you want to get it fresh before I handle my business the bathroom is down the hall on the right."

Parker stood still and favored a gorilla without the mist. Just dry. Ashy, black and decrepit. The 8 Track warbled the theme from Shaft and he began smiling and rubbing his belly. Vomit teased my tonsils and I walked out of the room. The messed up part is that he still had on his black ankle socks. Childish chuckles kept me company as I wondered how and why do I get myself into these predicaments. When I heard Parker singing the line, "He's a complicated man, but no one understands him but his woman..." I burst out laughing and hustled a bit faster to get to my car.

∞ *Nail It to the Wall* ∞

Why is it so difficult for people to understand the word no? No one likes rejection, but when someone doesn't want your ass it's an entirely different situation. Leave. Bye. Sayonara. Peace Out. Good Riddance. Hit The Road Jack. You Ain't Gotta Go Home But You Gotta Get The Hell Outta here on a really real type of move. I swear if Parker sends one more text, email or leaves a crying voicemail I'm going to shoot him in both of his ears. He's not using them anyway.

The last few days have been excellent until he calls. If you've ever been the reason someone has thought about or actually changed their phone number, you my friend are an asshole. And if you decided to call from a different number or blocked your number, kill yo'self. I'm seriously thinking about putting him into the Witness Protection Plan – I wanna murder his ass.

I listened to the first message he left and didn't bother with the rest. If you have to bother someone to make them bother you - don't bother.

"Wanda? Wanda? Pick up the phone! We can work this out! I have sex toys and I'll let you use them! Call me okay? Okay?"

What type of an ass is Parker? He's probably a cross between a stuffed one that's full of shit and one that just don't know shit. Damn...that's some kind of foul living if you ask me. Of course Pat couldn't wait until I got to work the next day to give me the 411 on him.

"Girl! You know he got fired from the limo company. He was late for work every day. That's why he showed up here. They let his ass go! He got escorted out the building and er'thang!"

"Well, good morning to you, too, Pat. And I'm not interested in hearing about Parker. I'm not seeing him anymore."

"Man, I know he's feeling bad. Got fired and dumped on the same day. I know you don't want an unemployed man."

"That's not the reason, but..."

What's the use? People believe what works for them and I had to leave it at that with Pat. I didn't say anything else and neither did she.

Right now Parker is sitting next to Lenword in her mind.

"Is anybody using the small conference room today at 2? I have a few proposals to go over with Kennedy."

A tooth whitening company should bottle Pat's teeth sucking skills. I know hers are a few shades lighter with all the air and spit she just let loose.

"Now what was that for?"

"I can't stand her fake ass. She's always looking at Jeremy when he comes here. I don't trust that ho."

"Pat, I'm sure Kennedy doesn't want Jeremy. In fact, I'm positive she doesn't."

"How do you know that? Bitches be lying."

"'Cause she told me I would never let him get this. He's too fat."

"What? Oh, I know she's lying now. She's just trying to throw you off the trail. Lying bitch!"

"Pat...is the room available?"

She swore every single lady wanted Jeremy. If she got it in her head that you wanted him, she automatically didn't like you. He must have a little Louisville Slugger between his legs.

"Yea, it's available. Make sure you keep that heffa away from me or else she's gonna have problems."

Her ringing desk phone prompted her to roll her eyes and turn and leave before I could respond. There is a God. Apparently the phone was for me because she buzzed me within seconds.

"It's Braxton, girl. Now that's what's up!"

I listened to Pat giggle before I answered. Damn good and plenty ho.

"Thanks."

Braxton and I talked every day since our first meeting. He made Parker seem smaller than he really was.

"Good morning, Braxton. How are you?"

"Good morning, Miss Luv. I'm doing great. And you?"

His voice wasn't deep but it sure managed to go deep and make a few things tingle in me. Horny takes everybody with her.

"I'm well. I'm looking forward to our dinner date this evening."

"That's why I'm calling; there's been a slight change of plans."

If he cancels with a lame excuse I'm gonna blast his fine ass.

"I have a last minute meeting and I know I won't get finished until after 8. How about you come by my place for a late dinner, nice conversation and a few adult drinks?"

Woooweeee, horny is ecstatic right now! Now I know good and damn well that I shouldn't go over to his place. We've only been talking a few days, we sort of work together and my legs can spread like Country Crock. Aww, hell, I'm cheap. Make that the store brand.

"Ahhhhh, Braxton can we re-schedule? How about this weekend? My schedule is clear."

"No, no, no. I want to see you. I have excellent kitchen skills and I promise to be a perfect gentleman."

Perfect gentleman? Shit, he betta touch my titties or something.

"Alright, you talked me into it. Give me your address and I'll be there at 8:30."

"Great! 7892 Walker Street."

"Walker Street? Do you live in a house over there?" Strangely enough Parker lived on Walker Street. I didn't bother to get his address, though.

"Yes I do. Don't worry. It's a good neighborhood and I live alone. My cousin was living with me until recently. He moved out last week."

Oh shit. "Uh, what's your cousin's name?"

"Parker Clarke. I got him on with a limo company but it didn't work out. Do you know him?"

"Yeah. We kinda talked a little bit but nothing came of it. I was at your house last week and nothing came of that either."

Braxton laughed until he lost his breath. I wasn't sure if I should be offended or join in.

"I'm sorry, Wanda. It's just that I *know* Parker. He's always looking for a free ride and you're just the type of woman he goes after. Beautiful, brains, and uh, a very nice body if I might add. I'm just glad that you didn't fall for any of his weak game. And don't worry – I'm nothing like him at all."

"Wow. Thank you, Braxton. Now I'm really looking forward to seeing you tonight."

"I gave him a lift to your office the day of our meeting. I didn't know he was going there to meet you."

"That was a disaster. Maybe I'll tell you about it one day. So I'll see you at 8:30?"

"Great! 8:30 my dear lady. See you soon."

"Bye, Braxton."

My mind immediately filled with thoughts of what to wear. If we had met out I planned to wear an off the shoulder taupe wrap dress with nude shoes. I think that might be asking for something more than dinner sitting at his place. I'll keep the pumps, but add jeans and a cashmere sweater. Hopefully my choice of clothing won't send a, "you can get it" message.

Loud laughter and a flamboyant voice quickly relocated my thoughts to the hallway. Mr. Harris didn't come into the office much but when he did a party wasn't far behind.

"Miss Wanda where are you?"

His you and my face met in front of my door.

"Hi, Mr. Harris. How are you?"

"I'm finer that flies on a shit cake!"

Mr. Harris thought everything he said was funny. When he found out I was a part time stand-up comedian he did his best to make me laugh.

"Good one, Mr. Harris, good one. I'm glad you're here. Do you have time to sign a few contracts? Things have been going very well, which means your business is booming."

"Well, hot, hot, hot devil damn! That's what I like to hear! Give me a pen! Let's get Bizzy!"

That honestly made me laugh. He made sure he used the word bizzy as much as he could. I've been with Bizzy Fiz for 6 years and I have an entire closet full of shirts, hats and jackets with Bizzy Fiz boldly printed on them.

"Please, sit in my chair. It's more comfortable than the chairs at the table."

"Do you need some new chairs?"

"Oh no, Sir, no. I just want you to be comfortable."

"You know there's no expense too big for my best Promotions Director. I'm so glad you came to us instead of going to Fiyah Productions. Since you came our name is all over the place. The out of state contracts are really picking up, too."

"Thank you, Sir. I really enjoy my job. Thank you."

"Oh, no, Wanda. This is more than your job – this is your family. Your review is coming up in 3 weeks and I think you'll be pleasantly surprised."

Asking was I getting a raise probably wouldn't be appropriate. Family or not, he was still my boss.

"All done! Wanda you're the best! Now to see the Misses and the boy and my day will be complete! I'll see you at the mixer, right?"

"I'll be there."

He tipped his hat and did a backward James Brown slide out the door. The rumor that he started is he went to school with James Brown and taught him how to dance. No one believed him because James Brown only went to school until the 6th grade. Sometimes the one piece jumpsuits he wears are high waters and tight. You can see his balls all scrunched up in the front. He still has his hair processed, but he really is a good man. Hardworking, a provider, doesn't stray; a prince charming in sequins.

"Hey girly, girl, what's up? Can I come in?"

"Yes, ma'am. Mr. Harris just left so I'm still on a 1972 high. He signed all the contracts, so we're all set to move ahead. How are things on your end?"

"On my way to listen to some new rappers. They want a video featuring hockey and Hennessey."

"Rappers?"

"Girl yes. Rappers. They think they can reach a new market. The song is called Skatin' on Thin Ice. Somebody is supposed to rob a bank, run into a hockey game and get shot."

"Tennille, you can't be serious?"

"You know Mr. Harris. Everybody deserves a chance. You want to come with me?"

"Naw, I'll let you handle this one. I need to finish up a few things here and get ready for my big date tonight."

"Date? With who?"

Tennille closed my door and hurriedly pulled a chair up to my desk. She flopped down, crossed her legs and readied herself for huge gulp of tea.

"Braxton."

His name flowed from my mouth like he truly belonged to me.

"We've been talking every day since we met. We were going out to Vito's, but he has to work late and invited me over for a late dinner."

I stop talking and Tennille almost fell out of the chair.

"Get this... that he's going to prepare."

"Awwwwwww, shit! You gonna give him some ain't you?"

"Tennille!"

"Don't play that Miss Delicate game with me. He is fine and you ain't had none in a minute. Somebody gotta get it. Pussy ain't no good unless it's in use!"

"I can't stand you!"

We laughed, took a break and then laughed some more. Tennille and I met in college and have been road dogs for the last 20 plus years. She got married to her college sweetheart right after we graduated and has been married ever since. They have 3 daughters and the life that a lot of women want.

"Tennille I can't give it up on the 1st date. What if we don't get along? I'll still see him and I'm not trying to go through that again. Remember Jeffery?"

"Yea, but he was crazy. Calling your phone at all times of the night and sitting outside your apartment; that fool was mental!"

"Braxton can't be like that...he just can't. But I'm not giving him any ass tonight. Horny is going to have to wait in the car."

"Alright. I'll let you slide this time but if you keep seeing him I want to hear about some sexual healing in the next 30 days. Deal?"

"30 days?"

"Wanda how old are you?"

"42."

"Make that 15. I'll see you in the morning."

When she swung my door open Pat's nosey ass damn near fell inside. I know she had her head pressed up against the door.

"Oh, uh, hey yah'll. What yah'll doin'?"

Tennille cut her eyes back at me and twisted her lips. "Nothing, Pat. Bye."

Rolling her eyes came naturally for Pat when it came to pretty women. She also thought Tennille wanted Jeremy as well.

"What's up, Pat?"

"So you're going over Braxton's house tonight?"

Why this little dog nose snooping bitch! She should be on a shit sniffing squad.

"What?"

"I accidently hit the conference button when you were talking to Braxton and uh..."

"Well why did you hang the fuck up? Damn, Pat, that's some foul shit right there."

"I'm sorry, Wanda. It's just that Lenword asked about you and I didn't know if you were single or not."

"So instead of asking me you listen to my convo? Get outta my office before I slap you. You're ridiculous sometimes."

Of course she wasn't wrong so she sucked her teeth and slowly sashayed out waiting for me to stop her. It bears repeating; some bitches are just bitches.

By the time I arrived home I had calmed down. From now on I'd check my line when Pat transferred calls to me. She was Mr. Harris' niece and wasn't going anywhere. Thinking about the reason she upset me helped a lot, too. Braxton. It was nice to be excited about a fine man. One that could cook or couldn't, but maybe enjoyed doing it was a plus. We wouldn't eat until after 9 so I made the hunger saver sandwich – Peanut Butter and Jelly, showered and watched Sanford and Son reruns before heading over to his house.

This time when I pulled up I surveyed the area and noticed the front of the home. It was very nice. A one story brick house with window shutters, porch furniture and hanging flowers.

Nice for a bachelor. I rang the bell and was greeted with a hug and a kiss on the cheek.

"Wanda, I'm so glad you're here. Come on in and get comfortable."

"It smells delicious in here." I stepped inside to the aroma of sweetness and fresh flowers. A perfect combination if you're trying to impress me.

"Since we didn't make it to Vito's I decided to bring a little bit of Italy to us. How about Lasagna, garlic bread, tossed salad and for dessert, German Chocolate Cake? Not Italian, but still good."

We smiled and high fived each other. So far, so good. Braxton had on a dark green button down shirt with black slacks. He took the light jacket I wore and went to hang it up in the closet.

"Wait right there. I want to give you a tour before we eat."

He turned and I gave him a quick up and down without him noticing. His hair was low cut and his beard was shaded and trimmed very neatly. His hands and nails were cut low and clean, and he wore a bracelet on his right wrist. I paused in the moment and let my eyes travel down his body to his feet. Since it was his home he had the right to walk barefoot. I don't know if the things I saw attached to his body were feet, though. My heart began to beat a little faster as I stared at them. Rocky Horry Picture Show for Feet. Night of the Living Dead for Feet. You will never imagine my horror when I saw his feet. What the fuck are them thangs? They looked like they didn't belong on him. The more I tried not to stare the more I looked. They were darker than the rest of his body, scaly and his toe nails were black. We were standing on carpet but the area in front of the closet door was bare. I heard a clicking sound when he stood there. This muthafucka has long dog nails? Naw, hell naw. Wolf nails is a better description.

Tick...tick...tick...tick...once he was back on the carpet the sound stopped. Them thangs should've gotten snagged in the rug. Shit...

"Come'on, Pretty Lady, let me give you a tour."

Braxton took my hand and led me throughout his home. I didn't hear anything he said nor did I pay attention to the artwork or sculptures he showed to me. All I could do was steal glances at his feet. Sasquatch. The Big Foot. I should call the authorities because I just found something that's on the unexplained sighting list. Fifty percent of his home was carpeted and the other was hardwood floors. When he stepped on the ceramic tile in the bathroom I thought Mr. Bojangles was in the middle of opening night on Broadway.

"Your home is very nice, Braxton. Thank you for the tour."

"You're so welcome. Now let's eat!"

Tick, tick, tick, tick, tick, tick. He jogged down the last few stairs and the Fourth of July exploded. Firecrackers, fireworks and cherry bombs. Am I too superficial? How could he be so fine and not care about his feet? One thing is for sure – I will not get naked tonight. If I have sex with Braxton horny will need caution tape around her. A police investigation will surely follow with the scratches his nails will leave. I'm so aggravated.

"Sit here, Wanda."

Braxton pulled my chair out for me and seemed so excited. He talked about his day, his meeting, and went on and on about the entertainment business and how it has evolved. Nice guy, a real nice guy. Do nice guys finish last? No. Nice guys with fucked up feet do. I'm here so I might as well enjoy it. I'll get to know him. Maybe we can work on his feet. The lasagna is good but if he says I put my foot in it I'm going to run out the door. Damn...

∞ *The Childhood Files* ∞

You're an adult much longer than you're a child, so childhood memories remain with you your entire lifetime. Parents should keep this in the back of their minds as they make decisions for their children. Do they? Nope. That's why some of us are just plain old to' up today. We just won't or can't let things go! It's hard to forget when all you can do is remember.

My issue may not be much of an issue with the state of the world today. My own inner turmoil that I must release at some point to heal is my lustful adoration of Vanilla Wafers. There, I said it! It's out and time to move on!

Why have I held onto this for so many years? I'm 42 and this one memory keeps popping up. Wanda, it's just a cookie. NO IT'S NOT! It's the cookie that my mother NEVER let me have! It's the cookie that only entered our house on special occasions. Since when did making a Banana Pudding overrule the hunger pains of a child? Ma why? Why couldn't I have the damn wafer? Why?

The mere site of the yellow box, the thought of the sweet taste as I nibbled; the feel of the delicate crumbs....aaaaaaaah...Did I get to savor these things? No! See, if my mother had given me one cookie, just one cookie, she wouldn't have enough to complete her masterpiece. Hell, it wasn't as if the lights or the gas would get turned off if I ate one. We wouldn't have to live on the street over one cookie. I love Banana Pudding, but I hate what it has done to me. I wanted to flip the finished product over onto the floor and scream, "Fuck you ya yella tasty mess!" I wanted it to feel like I did. Hurt. Upset. Mad.

When I go to the grocery store I always speak to the Vanilla Wafers – "What's up my, Nilla?" The box smiles at me and wishes me well. I don't always buy a box, but when I do, the wafers don't stand a chance at becoming the main attraction in any other delectable dessert. They are all mine! Awww, Lawd, talk about overdose issues!

I bought a box of Vanilla Wafers last week. It was then that I decided to write this and hopefully get over my childhood issues. I don't know if it's working. I can see myself standing in the kitchen begging for a cookie and I'm still mad! What is wrong with me?

They say the first step to recovery is admitting that you have a problem. I don't know what the second step is. I do know that I'm going to eat every damn Vanilla Wafer and think about the times that I didn't get to eat them.

It's a cookie. Think before you speak to your child. So what they spill something; will the house disintegrate? No, and you won't either. I have a little list that isn't written down, but I have to let it go:

1. One can of Cranberry Sauce on holidays. Uhm...Cranberry Sauce is only available on the holidays? Ma, why? Why, Ma?

2. Why did I get a whoopin' when I fell off the bike and chipped my tooth? My knee was busted open and blood was running down my leg. I was already one step from the grave. Ma, Daddy, why?

3. Why did we have to eat fish with the bones in it and get yelled at that we better not choke on the bone? Should you really have that

much pressure on you at the dinner table? I just don't get it.

Yeah, I got issues. That's why my fatass over eats every chance I get. A cookie? Thanks, Ma.

Hi, my name is Wanda and I'm a Vanilla Wafer-Aholic. I guess writing this didn't help. Oh, well, I'm coming to join you my Nilla!

∞ *Shake It Well* ∞

You can tell a lot about a man if you pay close attention. Watch the way he walks, the way he chews, the way he moves his hands or sits, and his facial expressions. No man is one hundred percent "hard" and they shouldn't be. It's the ones who hide the "softness" that you should be concerned about.

Braxton and I talk daily and he's a really decent guy. Still, his feet have me feeling some type of hurt way. I know I shouldn't let one thing, in this case two, turn me off and I'm really trying to focus on the good he has to offer. He's very well educated, financially fit, and stable, and has no excess visible baggage. Those Cyclops feet, though? Ugh. He probably waxed Noah's Ark with them.

I haven't seen the culprits since nor have I been back to his home. Our dinner was fun with fantastic conversation. To top it off Braxton is an excellent cook. I left his home around midnight with a peck on the cheek. He stepped in close to me and no doubt wanted to kiss my lips, but had to adjust when I pulled away at the last moment.

His foot grazed my shoe. Stabbing chills ran up my leg. I'm not giving up on Braxton; he enjoys me and I'm looking forward to what may happen between us. I just need to figure out a way to address his feet without hurting his feelings.

Pat called out sick today and her sister is her replacement. She isn't as non-professional as Pat, but she isn't much better. Hiring family isn't always a good thing. Praying, I buzzed her and hoped that she didn't come with extra sass this morning.

"Donella will you come into my office please?"

"Uh, right now? I'm on a coffee break. Can you wait a few minutes?"

Here we go…"Yes. Just come in when you're finished."

"I'll come in now since you already interrupted me. Give me a minute."

Donella's coffee breaks were usually a shot of Cognac with an espresso chaser. She was always wired and not worth a damn when it came to work.

"What's up, Wanda?"

Drunk ass. "Can you type up a letter for me and have a courier come pick it up? I have to get some contracts out."

"How long is the letter? I'm leaving early today for the Work Week Mixer this evening. I gotta get my weave tightened up. Are you going?"

"Yes I'm going and it's a one page letter. You need to do 5 copies with the attention to being different. Can you handle that before you leave?"

"Well, as long as you don't bother me while I'm typing I guess I can. I'll forward the phones to you to answer. Where is the letter?"

You haven't seen sorry until you've seen Donella. The only reason she works here is because her mother asked her brother, Mr. Harris to hire her. She was tired of her embarrassing them. One day she sat outside the Social Services Office with a lawn chair, laptop and a cell phone complaining about why she couldn't get food stamps. Just a messy fool.

"Here. Everything you need is in this folder. Thanks."

"Before I go let me ask you something."

I peered over my computer screen and really looked at her. Her blouse was halfway buttoned up and her titties were on the attack. They were pushed up damn near under her neck and covered in body glitter. Dried pork ass at a buffet table that no one would eat was more appealing. I bet when she took her bra off they dropped and looked like they had a stroke. Leaning to the side and slobbing for life.

"What is it?"

"Me and Lenword have been talking and he might show up tonight. I just wanted you to know in case you have any feelings for him."

Don't say shit...don't say shit...don't say shit...

"Okay, thanks."

She waited for me to say something else and didn't move for at least 30 seconds.

"Donella do you need anything?"

Anger caused her to slowly suck her teeth. She tooted her wide load up and turned and walked out the door. Lenword? Get the fuck outta here.

The Work Week Mixers were started by the Promotions Director that I had replaced. Bizzy Fiz wasn't a huge company, 80 employees, but you could go months without seeing someone. This was a chance to check in and catch up. My predecessor actually got fired after one of the mixers. He was getting it on with his secretary and took her in the men's bathroom at Bennie's, the restaurant they were at. Mr. Harris walked into the men's room and all hell broke loose. They could at least have gone into a stall. Dominick was sitting up on the counter with his ass in the sink and ol' girlie was doing the turkey neck gobble. The weird thing is that he had the cold water running down his crack. Some of the employees still talk about the hard and wet affair.

The mixer was set to start at six. Braxton said he would come, but I didn't want him to be my date. Deep down I really hoped he didn't show up. Usually various reps from different companies came – it was like our own little award celebration. Not that Braxton isn't a good guy or anything, it's just I want to see what I can see without him wondering who I was looking at.

Some people think it's good to date on the job, other's say never eat where you lay. I do spend a lot of time working or doing shows, so most of the men I deal with already have a connection to me. At 42 though I never thought I'd never be married, no kids and still working on the perfect career. Must be true that you get back what you put out. I've put out ass and it seems that's all I get in return. It's the type of ass that I have issues with. Dumb ass, broke ass, stupid ass, lazy ass, tired ass, sorry ass, cheap ass, lying ass, sneaky ass, hungry ass...damn. I feel like Forrest and Bubba right now; and that's all I gotta say about that.

"Hey, Miss Luv, what are you thinking about?"

"Hi, Jacob. What brings you down the hall to where the small people live?"

"Woman, stop it. You're hardly small. You know my father has tons of respect for you and so do I."

"I like that kind of talk. Come on in. What's up?"

"You're going to the mixer tonight right?'

72

"Of course."

Jacob is Mr. Harris' son. He'll give you anything you ask for – especially his dick. Jacob juggles a minimum of eight women at a time and has the nerve to call himself engaged.

"My cousin Vernon is in town and I kinda told him about you..."

I must look lonely.

"Kinda told him what, Jacob?"

Throwing his hands up in the air and then placing them on his chest was his white flag move. He is fine so I gave him a pass with his frequent flier mile having dick.

"I told him we have a sexy Promotions Director who'd be perfect for you. He's single, has one son from his previous marriage, and is looking to settle down and get married again."

"Jacoooob..."

"Come'on Miss Luv. You'll already be there. Just give the man a little conversation. If you don't like him no harm no foul. Please?"

"Since you gave me such a nice compliment and your father signs my checks, okay. Now as for you, will we have any trouble from your gang tonight?"

"Ha, ha, ha. Very funny Miss Comedian. Naw, no trouble outta me. I didn't tell my girl where I'd be tonight. I told her I'm working late."

"You know that never works with them. They can sniff you out anywhere."

"Well, you know I can put it on'em."

"Anyway...I'll see you later."

Jacob did a two-step out of my office. He is a pretty good dancer and that usually translates to the bedroom. If he's packing I can understand why the ladies go wild for him.

"Boy get your bootleg Thriller video ass out my way!"

"Don't knock it til you try it, T! Oooooooww!"

Tennille stood in the doorway snapping her fingers to her own beat.

"Girl what's up with you?"

"Jacob has me thinking about Thriller now! That fool! Are you all set for tonight?"

"Just about. I'm leaving in a few to get my nails touched up. Then I have to swing by the cleaners to pick up my red dress."

"Oh, shit! The red mini?"

"Yes, ma'am."

"Somebody is on the prowl tonight. Uh, is Braxton coming?"

After she said that she stepped inside and closed the door. I made a face to replace the words that didn't form quite right in my head.

"Are you still trippin' on his fucked up feet?"

All I could do was laugh and Tennille joined me.

"Wanda I think it's you. Your ass is too picky. Just make him wear socks all the time."

"Even in the shower? And I'm not picky; I just like what I like."

75

"Then tell him."

"We're not that close yet. If I keep talking to him he's gonna want to take it further. I can't see myself getting naked and his feet touching mine."

"Wow…are they *that* bad?"

"Ugh. Let's change the subject. Do you know Jacob's cousin Vernon? As per Jacob, I'll be his unofficial date."

"Now I get why Braxton is sitting in the shade tonight. I don't know Vernon but once I saw some of Mrs. Harris' family photos. If he's from her side don't get your hopes up."

"I don't think Jacob would do me like that."

The, I wish a muthafucka' would look appeared on both of our faces causing us to laugh again.

"Let me get up outta here. What time are you leaving?"

"Tim's picking me up at 5:30 and we're going straight there. I'll be there before six."

"Would you mind checking on Donella before you leave? She'll be good and lit by then. I just can't with her right now. She's so extra."

"Yea, go ahead and get ready for Vernon and Braxton's feet – I got you."

Tennille went towards Donnella and I locked my office and left through the delivery entrance. I was a little excited to meet Vernon yet I had some guilt concerning Braxton. Might as well be a grown up and get it all out tonight.

As I pulled up in front of Marigold's Restaurant and Lounge I saw Mrs. Harris stepping out of a limousine. 75 degrees and she has on a fur? I prayed that she had on something else under it. A tall, maybe 6'3" dark brown man began making his way to my car. I was sitting in the valet parking line, but there is absolutely no way he was a valet. Before my next thought could focus he was at my car door opening it.

"Wanda, hi, I'm Vernon. Jacob told me to look for the fine woman with the red Lexus. Allow me to be at your service."

Damn. Vernon can get it. Vernon will get it. Vernon...

"Oh, thank you."

He held my door open and I placed my hand in his. Just then a valet approached and Vernon handed him my keys. The smallest things mean so much. If a man pays attention and handles the little details I have faith that he will be on top of everything else. My body included.

"It's nice to meet you like this. Being escorted by a handsome man is a beautiful thing."

"Thanks for the compliment. Here, let me take your wrap."

I did a quick twirl while he held onto one end. I spun out of that thing like a stripper on a dick pole. Slick and ready.

"You look beautiful. Red is definitely your color."

We strolled in arm and arm and suddenly I felt like Blackarella at the ball. Champagne fountain, generous food platters, music and laughter. As long as pumpkin feet didn't show up it would be a good night.

Mr. and Mrs. Harris were on the dance floor gettin' it all the way in. Her fur was off and she was on a Tina Turner roll. She was showing her ass tonight. Silver booty shorts, thigh high silver boots and a lavender halter top were sealed with a curly soul glow wig. Mr. Harris had on a purple jumpsuit. It wasn't high or tight so his balls were probably bouncing all around. Love is a splendid thang.

"I guess you know my family loves to party. Ever since I can remember my aunt has dressed and danced like that."

"So you're a part of this clan from Mrs. Harris' side?"

"Yes, she and my mother are sisters. My mother is the quiet one. Let's grab a table over here."

Vernon took my hand and led me to a table for two that was closer to the back. We could still see the dance floor and much of the activity that went on. I didn't care if that scab foot fuck Braxton showed up on not. I can be such a thirsty heffa at times.

"So, Wanda, tell me a little about you. Jacob said you're a comedian among other things. That's fascinating to me."

Vernon waved his arm for a waiter.

"Would you like something to drink? I want to make sure you're comfortable."

Listen to my man Vernon. Uhmp...opening car doors, taking charge – love me in a special way, baby.

"Champagne will be fine."

"I'll have a double Johnny Walker Black on the rocks, please."

His mouth was sensuous. Mustache, goatee, thick lips. Celibacy my ass; I'm just a ho in remission. Vernon and I were able to get to know each other quite well considering all the interruptions. He was a music producer in LA and came to NY to check out a few of the groups on Bizzy Fiz. He was able to get that out between my dancing with Mr. Harris and listening to Mrs. Harris tell me about the first time Vernon played the drums in church. Tennille and Tim, and Pat and Donnella stopped by our honeymoon table also.

Lenword didn't show and Donnella was a dog without a chain. Whoever handled that for the night was definitely going to put in work. I'm talking broke back mountain bull riding work. She look swole and ready to release all of that love on whoever wanted it. Damn that's nasty.

Braxton called and I let him go to my voicemail. Vernon was at bat and I had to make sure he didn't strike out.

"I really enjoy talking to you but I want to dance. Come on, sexy lady, they're playing our song."

Montell Jordan's Get It On Tonight was blasting and the floor was packed. I'd had just enough champagne and was ready to work my red dress. Vernon knocked back 5 doubles of Johnny Walker Black. Either he is an undercover alcoholic or nervous. When he went to the bathroom I watched him glide across the floor to get there. He was a Denzel/Idris mix. Oh, yeah, Vernon would blow my back out and then some.

I placed my hand in his. After I rose up he slid his arm around my waist. Smooth operator indeed. Why we feel the need to walk to the middle of the floor to start dancing is beyond me but that's what we did. Once there it was on. Vernon moved seductively slow with the rhythm.

He took my hand and pulled me close to him and we swayed with the beat. He leaned in close to my ear and sang his intentions.

"Get it on tonight...you look so good tonight..."

Suddenly my fairy tale night came to a screeching halt. He stepped away from me and stood still. Gazing into my eyes as if some voodoo spell had taken over Vernon then turned his back to me. He bent over, and started shaking his ass like a straight up sweet bitch. That ass was rolling, dropping down to the floor and jiggling from side to side. Vernon's ass was delectable. You ever date a man that's so feminine you start to think you're a lesbian? Do I like women? Is that why I can't get a man? I couldn't stop staring. Vernon's ass was mesmerizing.

One minute he's a man's man and the next little ho peep? Is he a switch hitter? What the fuck?

To make it worse other dancers began clapping and yelling, Go, Vernon...go, Vernon... Men don't dance like that! Even men in the ballet don't look this swanlike. Once the crowd got involved he lost his mind. He was pladowing that

82

ass. He looked so nasty. I bet he has ass jelly on and it's sliding all around. My little two step is pitiful. I feel so dumb. What happened to my man? What the fuck?

My mind did flips as I watched the Johnny Walker Black version of Billy Madison. Would he want me to do things to his ass? Massage it? No, fondle is the word I should use. Smack it while we're having sex? What is his definition of freaky? If he wants me to stick stuff in his ass I can't do it. Does he own a pink pig? Look at him. What happened?

"Come on, Wanda! Shake it well like me!"

Shake it well? Naw, he's sending off a sweet tail tweet. Vernon is seriously rolling his ass. Can he make it clap? My eyes scanned the room and met Tennille's. She had her hand over her mouth. Vernon would be the topic of our conversation tomorrow morning. I'd make it my first priority after my sex-less night. No, hell no, I gotta think real hard about yo' ass and the rest of your body, Vernon.

∞ *Gummy Love* ∞

Driving into work this morning my mind was consumed with thoughts of Vernon. We, or shall I say, he, stayed on the dance floor for over an hour. I gradually made my way to the sidelines and he didn't notice that I wasn't his partner. He kept bumping and grinding and gyrating with the air, the floor, and whoever he came close enough to booty roll with. His dance fever was so nasty. A shot of penicillin couldn't cure it, but I'm sure he'd enjoy the needle prick in his ass.

Thankfully all concerned parties left the mixer before I did, which was around midnight. I was able to escape without being questioned about Vernon. Mr. and Mrs. Harris and of course Tennille would be the first in line waiting for my 411. Strange, but I thought it weird and normal that Vernon didn't call to see if I made it home, or call this morning, either.

I tossed and turned a bit and really didn't get any decent sleep. A presentation was tentatively scheduled for nine, and in order for me to keep my eyes open when the lights went dim I'd need a big shot of something good. Pulling into the drive thru of Caffeine Connections was my best bet.

"Good morning, Caffeine Connection. May I take your order?"

"Good morning. May I have a large caramel latte with 2 extra espresso boosts?"

"So that's a large caramel latte?"

"Yes, with 2 extra espresso boosts."

"Okay, will there be anything else?"

"No thank you."

"Your total is $6.49. Please pull up to the first window."

As I pulled around I remembered my interaction with the manager. Tennille and I came here for lunch a few weeks ago and she had hit on me. I think women are beautiful, but that doesn't mean I want one for my "girl". We were seated and she walked up to our table like we owed her something. She didn't say anything and slid her bootleg business card towards me. Then she winked, and asked me to call her.

"If you ain't doin' nothin' lata holla at me, aight?"

Tennille and I stared at her and I think I nodded out of fear. I watched her walk away and thought from the back she looked like a gorilla. Then I saw a flash of Parker. I've had enough monkey love. From the front you were greeted by her huge titbelly. I couldn't tell where her breasts ended and her belly began. Big shit for no reason. Her titties looked like someone peed on their bologna sandwich. Just sad. If I saw her naked I'd probably cry for fear of being suffocated. No women for me and definitely not a female brute with tits.

She wasn't at the window as I paid and received my treat. I inhaled my sweet concoction and began the sip that would make my night disappear. As I closed my eyes and thought of an isolated island I was interrupted by my cell. A private number? Grown folks who block their numbers are assholes.

"Hello?"

"Hi, Wanda...this is Vernon."

Vernon had the aura of a hard night of drinking all over him. It blasted me through the phone.

"Hey, Vernon. How are you?"

"Uh, I'm okay. I called to apologize and ask for another chance. Last night, uhm, I don't know what got into me. Maybe it was jet lag or nerves, or I just don't know, but I owe you an apology. I'm sorry."

A man who mans up without hesitation is a good thing. The booty shaking though? I still see his rump rotating.

"Apology accepted, Vernon. Things happen. Don't worry about it, okay? No harm no foul."

"Ahhh, man thank you. I was so worried that I messed up my chance to get to know you. Thank you. I'll be in the studio tonight with the rap group Iceberg. They have the new single Skatin' on Thin Ice and want me to listen to a few remixed tracks. I would like to take you to lunch, though. Are you free?"

87

"No, I can't today. I have a lunch meeting with 2 executives from The Paper Pages Group."

"Alright. Well, can I give you a call later tonight? I really enjoyed the time we spent together. I think I have to give up Johnny Walker Black, though."

That made me laugh and he joined in. Maybe Vernon wasn't "sweet". Still, the vision of him working that ass caused so many illicit thoughts to run through my mind.

"That'll be fine. Any time after eight is okay."

"Thanks, Wanda. I'll talk to you then."

Usually I connect my blue tooth before I leave in the morning but today I didn't. I pulled over when the phone rang and had been sitting in the Caffeine Connections parking lot talking to Vernon. As I pulled off I saw the manager, beastie titties, walking towards the door. Ugh, some shit just ain't right.

There's always something going on at Bizzy Fiz that sometimes shouldn't be. This morning it was Pat trying to finagle her way onto the video shoot for Skatin' on Thin Ice. She wanted to be a Set It Off type character. My vote was yes; shoot her ass and make her shut up. It was okay with me even if it was only for 3 minutes and 28 seconds.

"Sy I can roller skate, so I know I can ice skate! You can have me in a slow motion shot! I have a gold wig; it'll be hot!"

Symon is the choreographer for most of our videos. Pat had him hemmed up between the copier and the shredder. When he saw me his facial expression changed from one of desperation to gratitude.

"Morning, Sy. Did I interrupt you?"

Pat shouldn't have any teeth with the way she always sucks them. I know she's blown a few men dry in her day.

"Miss Luv...Miss Luv! I'm so happy to see you. Can we chat in your office for a few?"

"Yes, sir! Come on in!"

He made a face towards Pat as he slid from his outdoor prison. I could tell she didn't like it by the smoke that came out of her ears. Of course she

turned towards me and gave a pork rind lip curl –
crisp and hard. The rumor is that Jeremy got it on
with her cousin Hilda, which is short for
Nyeashahilda, when he was suspended from
work. Hilda lives next door and oooweee, their
story is too hot for Maury. Pat has been stank
towards everyone who mentions Jeremy, or who
doesn't give her what she wants.

"Thank you for saving me! Pat is still a
trip…she's a mess."

"Uh-huh. You didn't say that when she
was stroking your meat in your office. You know
that's your girl."

Sy took a step back and resembled a male
mannequin. He always did that when he felt
offended.

"Now why did you have to go there, Miss
Luv?"

"You know Pat has a *thing* for your *thang*.
You had that girl acting a fool for more than a
minute."

"Yea, I did, didn't I? But Pat is too easy.
She gave it up the first day we met and topped a

brotha' off real good. I don't want a woman that easy. Now you on the other hand…"

Symon and I dated for a few months. Nothing ever became of it because he was in the middle of a divorce that never happened. He'd take me out and then go home to his happy family. When I found out I roasted him in one of my routines and we didn't talk for a while after that. He apologized and we've been friends since. He says he's happily separated. Please…for him that means he's at work and she's at home. Sy is a nice man who ain't shit. Do nice and shit really go together, though? I've heard someone say, "I just took a nice shit." I guess it's nice because you're not bound up by it anymore. Anyway…

"What's up, Mr. Symon? You must need something if you're in our office knowing you can't avoid Pat."

"You know me so well. I came to ask if you'd like to come to lunch with me. I need a high ranking pretty individual who can sweet talk a client."

"Go on…"

"I want to do a dance shoot in Mr. Tan's restaurant and..."

"The one with the waterfall?"

"Yes, the one with the 5 story waterfall. He doesn't want to close down for the day. I need someone to explain all the exposure he'll receive from being in the video, which will lead to mega cash in his pockets."

"I can understand his hesitation. I mean, some of his entrées are $75 and up. Are you sure you need it for the entire day?"

"100 female dancers in thong bikinis? Hell yeah I need it for the whole day."

"Sy?"

"No, Wanda, this is a   seriously, serious business deal. This is gonna be hot! Have you heard the new single from Kerry Swerve called, Tasty Spot?"

"Oooooh that song is nice."

"We're talking a lot of money with this shoot. I gotta get Mr. Tan's. I'll get back on Mr. Harris's good side then."

"You just might if you stop screwing his daughter and act like a married man."

"Shit, tell her to stop opening up her legs and I will."

Sy is the first male choreographer who I've met that is all man. More like man dog. He'll stick his thang in any woman who'll have it. I didn't give it up. Sleeping with Sy changes you from a ho to a stank ass ho.

"What time is lunch?"

"How about I come back and get you at one?"

"Oh, wait, I can't. I forgot I have a lunch meeting with The Paper Pages Group. Can you do it tomorrow?"

"Wanda, we're talking dollars...Mr. Harris's dollars..."

Mr. Harris loves money and loves to give huge bonus checks to his employees.

"Alright. I'll reschedule with them. You betta not mess this up."

"Mess it up how?"

"Don't have none of ya "boys" getting sexed in the waterfall when the cameras aren't rolling. You know how you do."

"I promise I won't. I promise."

"Okay, I'll see ya at one."

"Thanks, baby girl!"

He slid across my desk and kissed me on the lips. Slick fucker. No sooner than he left my office Pat appeared. I did feel bad for her but I didn't want to hear about it – especially since I had Vernon and Braxton on my mind.

"Hi, Pat. Can you get Paper Pages on the line? I have to reschedule our meeting?"

"For what? You going out with Sy?"

The only thing that stopped me from stabbing her was a vision of me on Cops.

"I'm going to a business lunch with him. Is that alright with you?"

"You know he's married, right?"

"Can you get Paper Pages for me please?"

I have issues with my own fluctuating weight and really don't like to talk about big women, but Pat was turning into a mega fatass. Donella had sent an email asking for everyone to pray for Pat during this trying time. Included in the email was how Jeremy had moved out and Pat was eating to calm her nerves. When she turned to leave the linty stretch pants she wore clung to the crack of her ass. They were Grand Canyon clinging in her crack – wide, deep and rugged. Fatass.

When she left I closed my door and prayed for no interruptions. Paper Pages, although eager to meet, agreed to a breakfast meeting at nine tomorrow. With that out of the way I was able to buckle down and plan a few more promotional events that we had coming up. Mr. Harris decided to have his 9am meeting via email with Power Point attachments. He requested a reply and set up a lunch meeting for the coming Friday at eleven. Just as I was about to click save on an Excel chart, my cell rang. Mr. Can't Get On The Good Foot Braxton would not be denied.

"Hey, Braxton, how are you?"

"No, the question is how you are? I didn't receive a return call last night or this morning. What's going on, Miss Luv?"

"Well, I got in late from the mixer and this morning has been busy."

"Hmmm...you're never too busy for what you want. Now what's really going on?"

Damn, Braxton was a good dude and didn't deserve to get treated like clearance sale items. We were in the beginning stages, but is honesty always the best policy?

"Braxton, listen...uh, I really want to get to know you and..."

"So get to know me. What is it? Are you in a relationship? Getting out of one? Tell me what I'm up against and I'll knock it down. I'm digging you, Wanda. Corny yes, but you give a brotha' butterflies that wanna be caught by you."

Shit.

"Is it me? Just tell me what's holding you back? Please tell me."

Shit.

"I know you want a successful career and I want that for you, too. I'll support you and one day even love you. What's up, Pretty Lady?"

Shit. Honesty it is.

"Braxton I appreciate that you want to get to know me. I can be very superficial at times and I have issues."

"We can work through it. What is it? My breath? My feet? What?"

"Your feet."

I closed my eyes and imagined that I was on stage.

"Your feet are kinda f-ed up. They're what's stopping me.

Shark tales...jaws...fintastick...what is up with your feet?"

"My feet? What's wrong with my feet?"

All of a sudden I wanted to slap myself. His voice became so weak, but his feet are fucked up. Might as well let him know.

"They look like they belong on a wild beast. I can't lie down next to them. And laying down will happen at some point if we're in a relationship."

"Wow. My feet are that bad?

"Braxton your feet are fucked up. Sorry..."

Silence followed my harsh comment and then a few giggles. There were a few more giggles and snorts and then he let loose. I moved the phone away from my ear due to his loudness. Damn, laughing at yourself is good for your soul but this was a bit much, even for me.

"Uh, are you okay?"

"Wanda, you definitely are funny! You had me going there for a minute! Is this one of your jokes? Girl, you got skills!"

He continued to laugh and grew louder. Braxton had me on his side a few minutes ago. He can't think I'm joking...he just can't.

"I'm not joking. You have cling on feet. Them shits will cling on and tear up everything they come into contact with. You should wear dryer sheets for socks."

He dropped his phone and continued to laugh. I started to laugh, too. I hope his laughter wasn't a defense mechanism and he snapped later on. If so my black ass would end up on an episode of Black and Missing in America. He managed to compose himself as if what I said didn't pertain to him.

"Can we meet and talk in person? I know you're keeping something from me. How about I make good on the dinner date I promised you? I take you somewhere nice. Have you ever been to Hollandaze?"

I didn't know what to say. Should I state my case and let him know that I was serious?

"You don't owe me anything."

"I want to see you and get to the bottom of this. Let's make a date, okay?"

Your feet are the bottom of this.

"Can I give you a call later? I need to check my appointment book. We have a few events coming up this week and..."

"Oh, so we're back on the too busy thing."

"Braxton, I promise I'll call you."

"That's all I can ask, Pretty Lady. Talk to you soon. Bye."

"Bye, Braxton."

Did I really just have a conversation with someone, dog them, and they still want to take me out? When I get back from lunch Tennille and I are going to have a serious talk. I need some inside scoop on Braxton.

Sy and I arrived at Mr. Tan's shorty after one. When we entered I thought I had been transformed to some type of fantasy swinger flick. The waitress' had on tiny red edible bikinis and the male waiters could get it. Fine hot meat all up in my face. Mr. Tan was playing hard to get by the looks of it. He really wanted us to shoot there and gave an early glimpse of how things would look. Damn...maybe I should ask for a part in the video.

"Sy! Welcome!"

I'd never met Mr. Tan but had heard many things about him. He loved everybody's money, other men's wives and didn't care how he got what he wanted. I made sure my candy apple red lipstick was glossed up and ready for his imagination.

"Hey, Mr. Tan. This is Wanda. She's in charge of Promotions at Bizzy Fiz. She agreed to help me help you...if you know what I mean."

Mr. Tan looked me up and down. If he asked me to turn around I'd dive on Sy and choke him until he was burnt cheese black. Mr. Tan was in his late sixties and had more than crow's feet. When he smiled his eyes disappeared and his face resembled a grid of tick tac toe games that had been lost.

"Well hello, Wanda. Come over here and have a seat."

He snapped his fingers and an almost naked Nettie appeared. If the cops bust up in here we're all going to jail.

"Lela bring us a bottle of Moet. This is a celebration!"

"So Mr. Tan are you going to let me film here?"

"Yes! I've thought about it and I think it will be good for business. The word is out about what good work you do over at Bizzy Fiz and I want a piece of the action. Here, look at the menu and order whatever you want – it's on me!"

Tupac blared throughout the restaurant. How do you want it...how do you feel...I can't stand it when an old bastard has déjà vu.

"Come on PYT and dance with me!"

Sy looked at me, shrugged and began opening the bottle of champagne all the while smiling. Hey, if all I had to do was shake some ass for a whole lot of money I was way ahead of the game. Everybody is a prostitute for something in their life.

Mr. Tan pulled me to the middle of the floor. Everyone does go to the middle before dancing. I thought of Vernon, shook it off and began snapping my fingers.

"Awww, shit now! You got some moves, girl!"

Actually, Mr. Tan was getting his in. His old ass had on evergreen gators, a lime suit and a red shirt. He started singing and I started stomping my feet in an effort to encourage him on.

"Now tell me sweet baby if it's cool or what, tell me if it's cool or what... nanananananananan...you know what I want..."

He leaned forward and when he leaned back and smiled he gave me a mouthful of gums. His damn teeth fell out! He slid his tongue around his mouth and burst out laughing.

"Awwww, thit! I thused Pwepawation H stead' o'my Thenture Cweam this mornin'!"

I'm on the floor with a gummy mofo whose breath smells like ass? Where is my camera? I looked over at Sy and he was deep into a conversation with Nettie. What made me laugh is that Mr. Tan didn't even stop to reclaim his teeth. He kept dancing, smiling and singing. Nobody would believe this shit.

"Thumin' up in tha cath thame I'm foreal..."

This can't be. He began waving his hands in the air and all I could do was laugh. Looking at him made me realize if he was comfortable being himself without his teeth, maybe Braxton was comfortable being Braxton with his feet. Suddenly, I really wanted to find out.

∞ *Internet Bastard* ∞

Sy dropped me back at the office after three. Most of the ride he blabbed about how great the shoot at Mr. Tan's would be and I mostly nodded in agreement.

"Where is your mind at, Miss Luv? When you have that look on your face I know you're thinking about something."

"Men."

"Is that all I'm gonna get outta you?"

"Yep. And everything is fine. Just don't mess up the shoot."

"Okay...okay...and if you think long you think wrong."

After he said that I turned to him just in time to get his beautiful smile and a wink. Maybe I was looking too far into things. Braxton's feet were nothing to get upset about and so what Vernon is an undercover alcoholic. No big deal. Just my life. No big deal at all.

Luckily Pat was gone for the day and the office was quiet. Not that I needed more time to think wrong about anything, but I did need time to think. Funny, my mind couldn't concentrate on either Braxton or Vernon. I let it wander to a time when I tried internet dating. It doesn't matter where or how you meet someone, fake will show up when real has nothing to offer.

I joined a site called HusbandshereDOTcom. That shit sounds desperate, but a half a bottle of Henny on a rainy night with Patti LaBelle blasting If Only You Knew will make you do some desperate things. After hooking up my profile and searching the site I connected with a man named Peter Diggs. We chatted, emailed and after three weeks decided to meet. His face looked like his picture, but his body didn't. He was much heavier and round. Everything on him was round. Circular motion fuck.

We didn't make it halfway through our first date and I knew I'd never go out with him again. I'd probably never speak to him again, either. Two minutes after we were seated he asked me if I could cook. He quickly added that he liked to save money and if I could cook the same meals at home we'd stay in a lot. I'd cut him some slack for the sloppy belly hanging over his jeans and the high ass, but I don't think I could handle all of that and him being cheap. A cheap fatass? How can you be cheap and a fatass? That meant he would never contribute, but eat everything like he had a right to it. Nope, I couldn't do this. Peace out porkroll.

The next guy I met was worse. Dakar. He said his parent's named him Drake, but he felt Dakar was more seductive and would get him farther in his quest to become the next Denzel. Okaaaaaaaay...go for it playa. Living with your sister and her husband while doing it, and sharing a room with your college aged nephew? If being a damn fool was included in his quest he was off to a great start. Of course he didn't reveal any of this until we met.

When I saw him I knew it wouldn't work. Some men just look raggedy and dirty, no matter how hard they try. He said he had just come from an audition to play an auto mechanic. He looked everyday dirty to me, though.

"I know I look a mess, but I take my acting roles seriously. I've been working on cars every day in preparation for this audition. I wanted to make sure I looked the part right down to the dirty fingernails."

Suddenly computer dating didn't seem like the grand idea I thought it was. A couple mouse clicks tricked me. He was great behind the screen; if only I could hit control, alt, delete...if only.

Whoever decided that I was a great target for online dating should be shot. Advertisements for mature, attractive men looking for a great woman to settle down with reeled me in one Friday night. The one thing I wanted to avoid - ignorance, will get its point across via text, email, telephone and chat box. Online dating is definitely not all it portrays itself to be. Then again, it's not online dating per se, but the people. Dumbasses take it to a donkey kong losing level. Out of control loose ass dropping everywhere

Hi, Wanda. I checked out your profile and I wanna get to know you. If you an honest woman who don't play games I'm the man for you. I know you wondering how a good catch like me is single and I will tell you. I broke up with my babys mama cause she wanted to take me for child support. I ain't got no money. I told her no weapon formed against me shall prosper and I ain't paying shit. So if you wanna hang out hit me up so we can get to know each other. I can get plenty of women so I ain't gonna sweat you.

Peace,
Ralph

Stupid shit calls for a stupid ass response or better yet, no response at all. Ralph is a supercalifragilisticexpialidocious asshole. Why would any woman want him? A good catch? The sad part isn't that Ralph thinks he's all of that; it's that a woman somewhere will co-sign with his sorry ass. Men who don't take care of their kids don't need to see, think or get pussy ever again. HusbandsHere DOT com my ass.

My trek down memory lane prompted me to check the email account I'd set up strictly for online dating. It had been months since I was on the site. Besides, I had enough live activity going on. As I logged in I decided to delete it, but of course not before checking the 8 email messages that were waiting patiently for me. The first was titled, Im Yo Present. Yo? I didn't bother to open it and laughed instead. Everyone isn't a great speller and most people type the way they talk. I can hear him now, "Get yo ass up in here and give me some." Naw, I'll pass.

He emailed me 3 times with the same thing. Desperation is a mo'fo for real. The next one said, A Nice Guy. I opened it and my mouth fell open. A picture of Vernon stared back at me! What? I wasn't going to judge him, I mean; I was on the site, too. My picture was on my profile. Did he not remember sending an email to me? My name is the same, also. But then again, his name wasn't Vernon, it was Martell. His email was brief and to the point.

Hi,

My name is Martell Morris. I'm looking for a longtime commitment and I have a lot to offer. If you would like to know me please call and we can meet. I'm looking forward to hearing from you.

Martell

555-302-1966

Damn! The number he included wasn't the number he gave me, but it was a West Coast area code. Vernon...wait, I shouldn't jump to conclusions. Maybe someone else was using his picture. There are some strange people on the net. The chat light was on next to his name. I might as well make sure that someone was definitely using his picture before I make a fool of myself.

MissLuv: Hi Martell.

A few minutes passed before he responded.

Martell: Miss Luv! So good to hear from you. How have you been?

MissLuv: I'm great. Before I continue I have to tell you that you look like someone I know.

Martell: I hope he's handsome! You know we all have a twin.

Maybe this isn't Vernon after all. Unlike some people I look the same as I do in my profile picture. There's no way he'd talk to me as if he didn't know me.

Martell: I see you're on the East Coast. I'm visiting there right now for business. I'm a Music Producer and am checking out some local groups. Would you like to meet for dinner and drinks?

What in the hell is going on? This is some svengooli shit right here. This has to be Vernon. Doesn't this fool know he's talking to me?

MissLuv: Martell you look identical to a guy I met recently. His name is Vernon. Forgive me if I don't seem to catch on quickly, but this is definitely strange.

Martell: Wanda this is Vernon. I'm big into role playing and thought you were going along with it. I think it brings excitement to any relationship. Are you cool with that?

Hell no ya damn freak! Why can't people just be themselves? Are you that fucked up that you have to pretend? Grown ass man pretending to be some other shit? No, Vernon, I'm not cool with that.

MissLuv: Vernon I'm not into playing games.

Martell: It's not a game. And call me Martell when we're online.

Why this muthafucka here...

Martell: So I guess asking you if you're into swinging is out of the question, huh?
Swinging?

Martell: Do you even know what swinging is?
I can't even type right now.

MissLuv: Yes, I know what swinging is and no, I'm not into it.

Martell: See, that's the problem with so many black women. You don't want to explore and experiment. That's why me and my wife got divorced. I don't see anything wrong with orgies or two men trying something. She knew all about it. It wasn't like I was on the DL or anything.

I knew he was shaking his ass to sweet. Wow, Vernon is a free agent switch hitter.

MissLuv: Vernon, I'm sorry. I have to go. I'll catch up with you later.

Martell: My plans have changed for the night. I'm hanging out with some friends. I'll hit you up tomorrow.

He logged off before I could respond. Explore? Black women? Two men? I guess I'm an old fashioned ho 'cause I'm not swinging, role playing and definitely not watching two men. I should be glad I found out now, but what the fuck? Does Jacob know his cousin is warped? Sodom and Gomorrah is for real for real. Ugh!

Talking to Vernon made me feel some kind of nasty. Here I thought he was a nice, fine man looking for a healthy relationship. Man, he had me fooled without even trying. All I wanna do is go home and stare at the wall. Maybe it is me that's all wrong. Naw, hell, naw...you have to be compatible. Not being right for someone doesn't make you wrong. Shit, liquor store here I come. The only thing that can shake me out of this funk is a few shots of Henny and a whole lot of Luther.

∞ *We Need Instructions* ∞

Do you ever wonder why you never know the person you're in love with until you get to know them? Most of the time by then it's too late. You can't stand them at that point and realize you never liked them in the first place. You probably hate them and wish you could suffocate them with the blink of anyone's eye.

Is this the voice of a bitter woman speaking? No, just a wiser one. One that will no longer fall prey to perfect on the outside but... We all know exactly what I'm talking about. The one man that you wasted entirely too much time on. He says everything you want to hear and things you never knew existed. He tells you how the ones that came before him never loved you. Let's not forget his kind words of how he can make all the tears you cried before leave your memory without a trace. Now that's some type of asshole right there ain't it?

Lately, I've asked myself the question of how the one I thought was so perfect at the start, makes my stomach dry heave when I hear his voice now. Was I ever in love to begin with?

Why sure I was. I was in that version of he'll do for now until love. That love you know is wrong, but keep thinking it'll change to the halleluiah I's found my soulmate! Of course the blame falls on you. Admit it! Okay, but, still, some people know how to twist and turn your emotions the right way so in the end, you have no choice but to wanna kill their ass. How many times can an insecure man accuse you of lying, cheating, and insulting his character? What character you stupid mutha'fucka? A cartoon character? How many times in your life should you have to hear listen to me, do it this way or you're stupid, before you decide that you're dealing with a broken down jealous, game playing, can't get right selfish fool?

Do you ever wonder or ask yourself how much you've changed or given up to be with the one you "love"? If you have to do extra extra extra all the time maybe he's not the one. Ask the one you love the same question. If their answer is not identical to yours, you need to do some serious soul searching. I did; and that's why I'm sharing my thoughts with you.

One thing that gets me tight is this. Just because no one ever told you something about yourself doesn't mean it isn't true. Sometimes sparing someone's feelings isn't always the right thing to do. If they're having an off day in the breath area, let them know. I know a man whose breath smells like Assasol...Lysol that smells like shit. If you spray it the air will blow up. Damn. I wanted him to gargle with bleach and then die it smelled so bad. I'm getting mad now just thinking about it. The stankin' mouth fucker.

Just because a man has babies running around all over town, doesn't necessarily mean their penis is the stuff Mandingos are made of. Let me set the non-existent record straight – a penis can make a baby. A dick can please a woman.

The solution to my dilemma was simple. I let it all go. The only opinion of me that matters is mine. Let Mr. Tricka Pic Dicka (now you know that ain't yo' dick in the picture...stop playing) take his perfect baggage into another relationship and play with someone else for a while. I've had enough.

But then I thought; it wasn't fair that I had to go through it and the next person shouldn't have to either. I know mind reading is not an option, so I came up with a brilliant idea.

Every man should come with instructions. They should have a tag attached to their shirt pockets, so you can read all about what you're getting into. Hey, we read the instructions on appliances we buy, food labels, CD cases; what's the difference? I know it's a human being, but everything breaks down. That's the way life is set up. You're born, you live, and then you die.

I think it would be fair to read about their habits, their attitudes, and their sexual behavior. We need to know of the infamous impending day that they decide they need to find themselves and can't be with you any longer. You'll understand when they say baby I just need some time to see what's up with me and you. Of course they feel the need to spend that time with another woman, or two or three. Mutha'fucka please...

Oh what a wonderful world this would be! No divorce, no separation, no abusive relationships, no he said she said, no baby mama drama, and no having to deal with the family that's all up in your business.

Just think, you can avoid years of heartache, headaches, worrying, wondering and wishing you could click your heels a few times simply by reading a tag. Sound like a winning infomercial doesn't it?

Of course there will also be a side effect tag instructing you on how to behave when their attitude that day isn't what you expected. They may react a certain way ninety five percent of the time but decide to throw you for a loop the remaining five percent. Never fear; one small tag will prevent you from being the feature on Snapped. I feel for those women. Knowing a tag could have saved them makes me believe instructions would eliminate so many guessing games, and remove the words, huh, and this mutha'fucka here from your vocabulary.

True no one is perfect and the tag can be misleading at times. You may have an allergic reaction to him and never know it because the tag doesn't say so. Personally, shit, with heavy emphasis on the IT, after knowing what I know,

I'll take an instructional tag over a man that's packing and has only a daydream plan any day.

∞ *Reflections Of* ∞

An idle mind is more than the devils playground – it's a damn trash dump. Thinking about the past gets on my nerves. You can't change it, so why not embrace it, be grateful for it, and keep on moving forward? Jeff, one of my many I must be bored for the moment men ran through my mind for no reason and I got mad. Mt. McGreedy was his nickname. Always talking about eating. He went so hard with food he had his holiday meals planned out years in advance.

"In 2034 I'm gonna have sweet tea and pound cake at my Thanksgiving Dinner."

Da fuck kinda hunger is that? Jeff was someone I'd met through a friend of a friend of a friend. The problem was none of us really liked each other so Jeff was really someone's revenge.

Our first conversation should have been our last, but you know some of us women flip the nice card and lose every time.

"Wanda I'd like to take you out for shrimp, clam and lobster."

"Awww, thank you, Jeff. That's nice, but unfortunately I'm allergic to shellfish."

"Really? Wow, well you can eat some bread and butter, and get dessert."

Selfish fat bastard.

Boy I'll tell ya I've been on some exciting life changing dates that I'm finally going to take the blame for. When in doubt the answer should always be hell naw. Yeah, friends want to see you happy, but if you don't have any urge to have dinner or see them naked at some point why bother? Tyrone was another one of my, who fucked who to get you encounters. I met him at the damn grocery store. I read somewhere that you have to be open to meeting new people and one way of doing that is to talk to everyone you come across. A hello, how are you, or how is your day can possibly lead to marriage. Meeting a man while squeezing a lime might give him the visual of you rolling his balls and nothing more, though. Small chatter about the state of the nation led to the exchange of phone numbers, which led to dinner a few days later. Worst. Date. Ever. He's what I call a juicy mouth fuck. He talked about his ex and how horrible she was the entire time. Who wants a man that runs his mouth about a woman? She didn't cook well, she spent all of his money, and she was lazy and on and on it went. I skipped lunch that day and was hungry, so instead of slapping the shit out of him and leaving, I chewed, nodded and made a mental note to run him over in the parking lot. When he came out of the Dog My Ex 101 zone he had the nerve to say he really liked me and hoped we could go out again. Luckily I had a nice piece of ribeye in my mouth when he made his last statement. Chew and smile, Wanda, chew and smile.

One time I tried long distance dating. That didn't work for me. What man thinks you're gonna sit by your phone every night waiting for his call? And if he doesn't call he gives you the excuse of, "I fell asleep. " I'm sure you did, but at whose house?

Looks ain't everything, but everyone wants someone nice to roll over to. The first time you see someone you SEE someone, and then it goes from there. It's a plus if your mate is attractive and their parents look good, too. At least you're guaranteed a nice visual till death do you part.

Call me shallow if you like and I'll accept it. Distance and dog face aren't a good combination. Lincoln and I met at a business conference in Florida. Too much liquor and a dark room is a den for doubt. The ugly I saw was really there. I guess that's why I didn't give Lincoln a chance. He treated me nice, spent money without question and knew how to long distance kiss my ass, but Lincoln was a little on the facially challenged side. Dayum...I couldn't find one feature on him that I liked. Even his fingernails look like they've been digging shit since birth. Dirty nails are a serious turn off for me. Sliding your hands all over my goods and your nails are dirty? I could vomit right now thinking about it. The topper is his mama and his daddy look like some, "What's that right there," shit. I had nothing to look forward to.

I decided to take the morning off and show up at work when I got there. Thoughts of video vixen Vernon or Martell, made me toss and turn all night, and I woke up with a serious sour patch kid face. No sense in going to work making other folks miserable just because I can't get it together. I woke up early and stared at the ceiling wondering where my special person was. You know everybody – independent women included, wants that one special person who they can share everything with. Secrets become conversation and love becomes your life. Free-fall and they will catch you. Provider, protector and it's always all about you. Mutual affection with trust and no questions asked. One day my prince will come. I guess.

My mind raced forward to the date I really didn't want to go on. I don't think Marvin will be my prince, but I promised his identical twin sister Marva that I'd go. The things I do to promote Bizzy Fizz Entertainment.

I've done business with Marva for years and she's always pushed her brother on me. Today is the day that my rain check tickets have run out. Braxton is still on my to-do list, but I need a just because fun night out. Marvin is a nice guy and is attractive - even with his thick ass magnifying glasses. I'm sure he's sun-fried a lot of ants with them things. I hope his eyes aren't crossed underneath. Damn, if we do the electric slide he's gonna be all messed up. To the left, fool...to the left.

The extra few minutes I tried to get daydreaming were interrupted by my ringing cell.

"Hello?"

"Girl, where are you? There's a nice looking man in the front office with flowers for you."

"Hey, T. Nice looking man? What does he look like?"

"Tall, dark brown and muscular with a low haircut. He's aight, but his glasses are kind of thick. Who is he?"

"Haha...that's Marvin. He's the saleslady Marva's twin brother. Can't you see the resemblance?"

"Yeaaaaaaaah, now that you mention it I can. Marva does have male features. Thank God she doesn't have glasses like him, though. Girl, they must be bulletproof. Maybe you can fix him up and get him some contact lens."

We woman always want to change a man. He has to stop wanting to be blind for himself – not for me.

"Now there you go. Can I at least meet him first?   Besides, he may not be able to wear contacts. His might look like fish scales."

"Wanda I can't stand you!"

"I know, you love me!   Let me call him. I thought we'd meet at Club Diva and get acquainted there. I didn't know he would go in with the romance part."

"Alright, Lady. Will I see you later?"

"Yes, ma'am. I'll be in within the hour."

I called Marvin immediately after hanging up with Tennille. Before his hello I heard Pat flapping in the background. I wanna slap her so bad.

"Hello?"

"Hi, Marvin its Wanda. I'm sorry I missed you. You are so sweet to bring me flowers. Thank you."

"Oh hey, Wanda. You're welcome."

An irritating voiced blared in the background.

"How she know you here?"

Why can't the floor cave in where Pat is standing? She makes me sick! Just then Tennille saved him from Pat's lonely girl wrath.

"Hi, Marvin. I'm Tennille. I'll take those. Wanda will be in within the hour. Would you like to wait?"

"No, no, Marvin. Don't wait. Please leave the flowers with, Tennille. I'll call you in a little bit so we can have some privacy."

I can only imagine the bewildered look on Marvin's face with three women yapping at him at the same time.

"Sure thing, Wanda. I'm looking forward to our evening and I'll talk with you soon. Bye."

Pat said something that I couldn't quite make out. Loose mouth heffa. Knowing that I held the first place spot in Marvin's mind did make me feel better. Hey, everybody needs a little luv – even if its love disguised as love. Just gotta know how and when to tell the difference.

While I showered Raymond tapped me on my shoulder. I guess this is the day of my reflections. Now that fool was a trip to the damn Bermuda Triangle. Doomed. Raymond was one of those men who thought his looks could get him everything from woman. Sex, money, meals and wheels. Free reign because of decent DNA? Mutha'fucka please. Now I love a fine man, but what man is that fine? When he admitted to me that he had more faith in his looks than his brain and ability to get the job done oh hell naw slapped me in the face. Sometimes you see a person in the moment. Other times you look at them and see what they can become. To see potential in a man is motivation to make it work. Strangely enough when I look at Raymond all I see is shit. Backed up overflowing shit. I always closed, opened and blinked my eyes a few times, but nothing changed. He probably couldn't even help himself. It's sad to see tired shit.

The thought of Hershel followed Raymond. I'm glad that I didn't have sex with my potential husbands. I'd be a Jerry Springer type ho.

"Wanda if I had my shit together I'd marry you right now!

Me and my men and their shit.

"I mean right this second! I love you, girl! But you know sometimes things happen and everything gets messed up. Like I don't even know if I can pay my rent or buy groceries this month. That's why I'm glad I met you. You'll always have my back when I fall short of the Lord. And_____."

Fall short of the Lord? What? And who wants to marry into shit anyway? Is shit better together or apart? Regardless of where it is if it looks like shit, smells like shit and can't do shit its shit. This fool doesn't even realize that I've zoned out. I've known him 2 weeks and he's talking about marriage. A broke ass man will latch on to anything breathing.

"So that's why I think I should move into your place. I can start saving money for our_____."

And he's in the end zone again. Some folks you just can't with. Seriously, you just can't.

I don't like rejection, but I know a few folks who cannot stand it. Seriously you need to stop crying and complaining about what's not meant for you to have. That's life. People also have preferences, too. If you're not on the preferred list of likes move ya ass on. Calling me an uppity beeeeeeeeyatch and slamming the phone down might place you on my preferred rejection list. Just because I don't want to date a guy who is getting over a bout of VD and has his herpes under control doesn't mean I'm uppity does it? Uh, yeah, no - that doesn't make me uppity at all. When it comes to food, clothing, music, movies, LIFE, everyone has a preference. I prefer dark meat over light meat. That does not make me a racist. So dear white man that I've turned down at least 10 times it's not you, it's me. Damn...and for the record white boy, I'd prefer a 6 pack, 12 pack or even a flat 40 ounce to that 24 case you call a belly...everybody needs a little luv, but no.

Let me get up outta here and leave my past right where it is. I have a date with Marvin, and regardless of his glasses, I'm gonna focus all of my attention on him tonight.

∞ DUID ∞
This Page is My Stage

Flashing lights in your rearview mirror are never a good thing. It upsets everything that's supposed to be right in the world. Paying for rushing to be on time, or already being late will keep you fuming every time you think about it. No matter what the reason for the ticket, you'll always get mad that you got caught. Well, maybe there are a few exceptions. I got a ticket a few days ago and all I do is smile every time I think about it. Not because the cop was fine, either. Honestly I'll take a few tickets for DUID.

Many ladies have sped for it. Some of us have even sat outside in our cars on a cold day waiting for it to come home. We think about it all day long, wondering what it's doing. Praying that it only wants you. Yeah, a good one will make you do not so ordinary things. Drink an entire bottle of brown liquor and plot how you can get more of the D. Cry in public, think about committing suicide and whoop all kinds of ass. You just wanna plead your case to anybody who will listen.

We let a lot of things slide for a good one don't we ladies?

"You ain't got no money for food? You get paid tomorrow? That's okay, baby. Just come on home – I'll take care of you."

No good D? Please, your broke ass will starve.

"You got fired? Don't worry about it – we'll find a better job for you. Just come on home – I'll take care of you."

No good D? Get your bags and get your unemployed ass outta here. Can't fix shit, don't know shit, and just full of a whole lotta shit? Get up outta here with your shit...ah, but if you got the D? Haaaaaaaay...

The first time I realized that I had a problem with DUID was when I went back and read my diary entries.

Monday, April 3 – Dick is good.

Saturday, April 8 – I like dick.

Tuesday, April 11 – Dick, the other white meat. It's betta than fried chicken.

I know I can't be the only one. Why do we allow it to consume us? Walking around singing yabba dabba dicky will doo thinking about our late night treat; damn shame. Once I thought someone should come up with nursery rhymes for dick. We do act childish over it and a good one will put you to sleep.

Dick in the Beanstalk

Dick be nimble, dick be quick...neva mind, nobody wants a quick nimble dick.

The little old lady who lives in a shoe. She has so much dick she don't know what to do.

Snow White and the 7 Dicks

Dickerella. At midnight it gets huge and she loses her shoes and her mind.

I was near rock bottom when my doctor told me I had to give it up. I almost had a stroke due to my blood pressure being so high. I ran across a string of salty ones and well, it's hard to turn a good D down.

When you're not getting any fantasizing about D is really bad. One night I had a dream that Big D was running around the house with a green and purple D cape on. He vacuumed, washed the windows and made Beef Stroganoff in the crock pot. D is the man.

For now I guess I'll have to slow down and understand the true fact that I cannot control what goes on in D's head. I don't think even D can control that. Yeah, I'll gladly pay my driving under the influence of dick ticket this time, but if I continue to get DUID's rehab just might be in my future.

∞ *Huh* ∞

When I arrived at the office Pat was waiting for me with her lips poked out. All I wanted to do was see my flowers and get on with my day.

"Hey, Pat, what's up?"

"Jeremy asked me for a divorce! Can you believe it? After all I've done for his sorry ass he wants to give all of this up? Over my dead body!"

"Pat calm down. Come into my office so we can talk about this in private."

Have you ever cared about something and didn't give a damn about it at the same time? That's how I feel now. I don't wanna hear this shit.

Pat stomped inside my office and flopped down on the sofa against the wall. She's the reason why cushions get flat or burst. No type of respect for others people's property. Once she got comfortable she became the lonely lady at a funeral. Hollering and wailing for no damn reason at all. The person is dead and they didn't even know you. Bitch shut up. All I could offer her were some tissue and a somewhat sympathetic ear.

"Calm down, Pat and tell me what happened."

"Calm down? I can't calm down! I've been sucking Jeremy's dick for 8 years! And now some sorry bitch with gingivitis comes along and he doesn't want me anymore? What am I supposed to do now? Whose dick am I supposed to suck now? Huh? Tell me who?"

Did she say whose dick is she supposed to suck now? She's getting a divorce and all she can think about is sucking dick? The world is a damn ghetto for real.

"He had the nerve to say she was having his baby and he had to do the right thing! He should have kept his dick in his pants – that would have been the right thing! Stay loyal to your wife! That's the right thing you black congo beast mutha'fucka!"

I wanted to laugh so bad. Black congo beast? Lord give me strength.

"Pregnant? His rusty ass told me he couldn't make babies. Wanda, I want kids. I went and had my tubes tied because he said that would make us even. I've been such a fool!"

"What?"

"I love Jeremy. All of his faults and flaws are mine, too. I love him. I have worked with him to make our marriage better. I know he's not the best man, but he's my man. I want to grow old with him. He took our vows and just threw them away. What am I going to do now?"

And then she cried...and cried...and cried. And then she continued to cry...and cry...and cry. I sat there motionless, staring in awe and saw Pat as a woman. I saw her as a normal woman with feelings and emotions. And then I saw me. I saw someone who wanted the perfect relationship for herself. Flaws and faults included.

"Pat, I'm so sorry. I don't know what I can do. Tell me what do you need for me to do?"

"Just be my friend, Wanda. Just be my friend. I'm not the best worker and I haven't been the best to you. Will you still be my friend?"

Damn she looked fucked up. Crooked and clumped eyelashes; her ponytail was matted, and snot was clinging to her face more than her dollar store foundation.

"Yes, Pat, I can be your friend. Do you want to go home? You can take some time off if you need to."

"No! That fucker is laid up next door. Had the nerve to ask to borrow a bag of sugar last night. What the fuck happened to asking for a cup? He's a bitch ass!"

Pat was killing me. She was still sniffling, but boy was she hitting Jeremy hard in his balls. I know he was bent over in pain.

"Why don't you go into the conference room and relax for a while. It's okay, there are no meetings scheduled for today."

"Thanks, Wanda. I won't be in there long. Uh, can you give me the key to the employee cabinet? I left mine at home."

The employee cabinet was really Bizzy Fiz's liquor store. I didn't say anything as I handed her my key. Hell, she needed a little brown liquor after all of that. I sat back in my chair after she left and actually felt bad for her.

"Hello?"

Pats words jarred me. Braxton was a man who I really wanted to get to know. I began dialing his number before the door closed completely. Flaws, faults and all.

"Hey, Braxton. It's Wanda."

"Ahhhhh, the elusive Miss Luv. How are you, Pretty Lady?"

"I'm fine. Listen, I haven't been so nice to you and I'm sorry. Please accept my apology. Can we start over?"

"Yes! Yes! Yes! Do you want to start right now? I can be there in 30 minutes or less. I deliver!"

It's the little things that send me into orbit.

"Hahaha...no Braxton. Can we make a date for tomorrow night? How about we go to that restaurant and start off fresh?"

"What's wrong with tonight?"

"Weeeeeel, I kinda have to go out with my co-workers brother. It's nothing serious. She's been after me for years to go out with him and I have run out of excuses."

"Okay, I'll tell you what. How about you call me when you get home for some pillow talk?"

"Mmmmm, that sounds good to me. And Braxton, thank you."

"Don't let him kiss my lips and you're welcome. I'll be waiting for your call, Pretty Lady."

As I hung up I wondered was Braxton too good to be true. I always over thought things whether it was work or comedy and didn't want to start off with bad habits. I never had a nourishing relationship so I was ready to dive into unknown territory. Change is a wonderful thing. And what is it that they say about those "kept people" anyway? Those people who kept doing the same things over and over and expected different results? Shit, the one thing I don't want to be is a kept woman. A woman who kept giving up the ass...kept getting cheated on...kept trusting the wrong man...kept getting stood up...kept taking him back...kept crying over the same old shit...kept hope all the way alive...kept trying to change him...kept trying to change me.

Weird that I didn't notice them before but bam, right in front of my eyes were the flowers from Marvin. Googley eyes went in with his. 4 dozen red roses? I've never seen a bouquet this big before. That's an anniversary anal sex golden shower bouquet. I just wanted a chicken sandwich. This would be a long night.

A quick call to Marvin to say thank you and going down the hall to check on Pat is what I planned to do next. The police type knock on my door jarred me and halted my plans. The door swung open before I could ask the culprit to enter. Sweet cheeks stood before me in a blue velvet vest, a red blouse that was too frilly for a fool and tight ass black jeans. The fuck is this shit?

"Vernon. How are you?"

"I'm good. I just came to tell you that if you had plans of being in a relationship with me you might as well forget it. I'm tired of hiding who I am to please other people. I like women and I *love* men and if you can't accept that then it's over."

Some people think that you give a fuck, but in reality its fuck you. Go'head with ya bad self ya ass smashing bastard. A relationship? He's an asshole.

"Uh, okay, Vernon."

Asking if we could still be friends would make him think that I actually cared. Oh what the hell, play with his rump roasting ass for a minute.

"We can still be friends can't we?"

"Yes, and that's all we can be. I don't want you to get your signals crossed."

Like you got your signals crossed? Dick, pussy, pussy, dick, ass, ass, ass. Confused dummy.

"Okay, I understand. Thanks for stopping by."

Vernon stood up and walked back out the door, slamming it like he was ordered to pay 12 years of back child support.

Quickly I dialed Marvin. He answered with a heavy breath – the jacking off kind.

"Hi Marvin. Did I catch you at a bad time? You sound busy."

Uh, no, I'm not busy at all. I was just doing some exercise to get ready for this evening. I gotta look my best.

Shut up, Wanda. "Okay, okay...I want to thank you for the flowers. They're beautiful."

"Yeah, I figured you'd like them. Nothing is too expensive for my baby. I'll pick you up at 7. Is that enough time to get ready for your man?"

"What?"

"I said..."

"I heard what you said, Marvin. I think you're mistaken about the man/woman part. This is just a date, right? We're not a couple."

"Oh, I know, I know. You're supposed to speak what you want into existence. I'm just talking up our future. I hope I didn't turn you off."

"Oh, no, not at all."

Why do we women lie all the damn time?

"I have some things to do after work so I'll meet you there, okay?"

"That's fine. I made a reservation at Doc Rob's Sports Bar before we hit the dance club. Nothing too fancy. It's a nice place to relax and have good food and get married."

"Marvin?"

"I'm just joking! See ya later, baby."

Marvin hung up and I wished I'd cancelled the date. He sent off a desperation vibe. I didn't think he was crazy enough to jump me seeing I knew his sister and we knew many of the same people. Still, I think he's the type to set up a camera in a woman's public bathroom. Either I've torn another hole in my ass or I'll get away with a chicken sandwich. Might as well get on with my day and check on Pat. Knowing her, she's brown liquor full already.

∞ *This Mo'fo Here* ∞

On my way home the blinking light to Happy Spirit Wines and Liquors flashed its way into my heart. The only thing I had in my refrigerator to relax my mind was a flat wine cooler and that definitely wouldn't do the trick. I wasn't a big drinker, but nights like this needed a heavy hitter. Hennessey called my name like Switch. I call your name, Wanda. I hear ya, baby.

I looked forward to a fun quick evening with Marvin. The sooner our date was over the sooner I could see what would happen, if anything, between Braxton and me. Sometimes what you wish for is worse than you'd ever imagine. The date was awful and went quicker than I planned. I wasn't going to rush the man but damn. Horrible...just horrible.

Marvin's conversation or lack of made me think I was on a pornographic game show called Dicks Who Have Dicks.

"I'll take Blind Dicks for $200, Jim."

"Who wears magnifying glasses and is a colossal dick?"

"Who is Marvin?"

Ding, ding, ding, ding, ding! "You are correct!" I should run out of the door now.

Some men are just stupid. Dumb asses times one hundred. Marvin ain't had pussy since Liberace did. He couldn't have. A grown man who has some kind of restraint and respect for himself doesn't talk like that. He just can't. He's so horny it's ridiculous. 52 and wants some tail like a death row inmate who has five seconds on the clock wants a call from the governor. All he did was talk about what he thought he could do and make you do in return.

"Don't these mashed potatoes look like a fluffy ass?"

"A fluffy ass?" I really didn't want to know so in a low voice I asked myself instead of him what exactly is a fluffy ass? He told me anyway.

"You know a light skinned girl with a bouncy booty. You're not light skinned so you don't have what I'm talking about. You have a meatloaf."

I didn't know what to say so I thought of the conversation that I would have with Braxton instead. This muthafucka here was stupid.

"My sister told me you've been single for a long time. I bet you're ready for some, huh?"

"Ready for some what?"

"Some sex. Women over 40 can't get enough. You're behind in your supply so your man Marvin Mar is here to fulfill your need."

"Marvin Mar?"

"Yeaaaaah...let Marvin Mar handle your needs. See, Marvin Mar will make you want to have his baby. Marvin Mar will put this hard six inches inside of you and make you want more. Marvin Mar will make you call Jesus and beg for mercy. Get with Marvin Mar, girl."

Sorry, Marva, your co-worker Wanda has left the building. Marvin was standing up beside our table mimicking an asshole on a catwalk. Sometimes spit balls flew out of his mouth. Slobber mouth and six inches? It's time to sit your dumb ass down.

"Marvin, you're an asshole."

I guess he thought someone told him something wrong. That would explain the startled look on his face.

"What?"

"I don't know who you think you're talking to or what you expected but I'm not interested in any of the shit you're talking about. And referencing yourself in 3rd person is for idiots. Are you an idiot, too?"

"Wanda, I..."

"You know what, please don't say anything else. I only came out to meet you as a favor for your sister. I'm too old to do things that I really don't want to do. I can pay for my meal so you don't feel cheated."

The waitress magically appeared as I finished talking."

"How are you two doing over here? Can I get you anything?"

"Yes, I'd like a to-go tray and the check for my entrée."

A slick mouth woman always reveals herself by the way she pokes her lips and twists her neck. I know Marvin and I would come up in one of her conversations this evening.

"Can I get you a to-go tray, too, Sir?"

Marvin Mar didn't say a word. He stared at me with a pained look on his face.

"Sure, please bring him one as well."

Slick lips left our table and Marvin Mar let me have it.

"I have never been so embarrassed in my life! How dare you insult Marvin Mar in public!

Do you know how many women want this right here? Do you?"

People began to look towards us. I didn't say a word. I'd heard once that you should never interrupt a crazy person. If you do they get stuck in that level of crazy for life,

"No, Marvin, how many women want your six inches?"

He sat back in the booth and sighed. Then he made an inaudible sound and went to the men's room. I would bet money that it was the Fred Flintstone water buffalo yell. Bahahahehaw or some shit like that. Marvin is straight stupid. No wonder Marva kept trying to push his dumb ass off on me. Nobody wanted him.

I gathered my things and met our waitress at the register. She had a stank snicker on her face. Please, if the heffa only knew. She'd probably get Marvin Mar's six inches. As she contemplated how to get my man I told her to ditch the tray and let me pay the bill for both of us instead. $42.78 on Marvin Mar. Braxton better pillow talk my meatloaf ass full of gravy.

Happy Spirit's was packed. All I wanted to do was get something strong without being hassled. Honestly it's nice to get hit on, but after a while some men should just quit. There's no fun in the chase when you know you'll never catch what you're running after. I mean no, naw, hell naw, kill yo'self-please. NEVER. It really bothers me when the man that keeps swinging and missing is an old fuck. Raggedy mouth, dusty clothes, dirty shoes and the only care he has is if you'll give him a few dollars towards his Golden Ale purchase.

Every time I come to this store Mr. Dusty puffs up his chest. He gets ready for rejection and begging at the same time. One time Pat and I came in together and she knows him, which makes him think he knows me. I didn't feel like hearing moonshine muddy so I got ready to respond with stupid shit that he would understand.

"Gurl you need to think about some old man lovin'. It's real good."

He had the nerve to slide his hand across his pant zipper like he could really do something.

Old man love my ass. When an old bas'tid thinks he's doing something he's really pissing on you.

"No thank you. Old dicks get Alzheimer's. They forget what to do and just lay there limp instead."

Most of the store erupted in laughter. Another old bas'tid dropped his coins and cleared his throat. He'd been staring at me blouse and asked could he marry me next lifetime. Erykah Badu gave hope to the wrong man.

"You have a nice day, Wanda. Tell Pat I'll come by tomorrow."

Damn, if I can't get a man in this lifetime and he's what I have to look forward to when I die I'm more than a little bit fucked.

A warm bubble bath and a little Henny on the rocks would get me nice enough for Braxton. My choice of drink wouldn't cause me to have skank mouth chatter that would lead to me asking him to come rock me tonight for my horny ass sake. However, it would relax me just enough to talk to him with an open mind and let him into the fun side of me.

After exiting my bath I continued to set the mood for my delayed booty call. Scented jasmine candles and Luther singing low in the background set it off. Please don't let me become a hoe without a cause. Three rings passed and my insides tingled.

"Pretty Lady, Pretty Lady, Pretty Lady. I've been waiting for your call. How are you?"

Uh-oh. I haven't had sex in three years. Braxton's voice made my nipples hard. Uh-oh.

"Hey, Braxton. I'm fine. Relaxing with Luther and you. I'm just fine."

"Ahhhhhh, Luther, my favorite. Can I sing a little something for you?"
"You can sing?"

"Don't sound so surprised, Pretty Lady. Along with my business savvy mind I can blow a karaoke session out of the water."

Oh hell no. I know he wasn't about to tear up Luther. I understand that he was trying to be endearing but fuck that shit. It's Luther.

"Put on Superstar and turn it up a bit."

"Superstar?" He can't be serious.
"Wanda, trust me."

I did as my maestro requested and then waited to hear a vocal disaster. Braxton began singing and my bedroom transformed to one that held a woman in a romantic movie.

"Long ago...and oh so far away...I fell in love with you..."

What?

"Don't you remember you told me you love me baby..."

My lips were pressed to my glass due to the fact that I couldn't move. I wish I had told him that I loved him. My mind raced with thoughts of us in our younger years. We were married and had two sons and a dog. Our life was beautiful and peaceful. It would be during one of our family nights that I'd turn to him and tell him that I loved him. A stupid but loving smile would follow. If I had done that in my mind years before I wouldn't feel like the slut that's trying really hard to interrupt me right now.

Braxton continued to sing as I sat in silence. He moaned and gave me ooh baby love groans as if he had won a Grammy. My body grew hot with the thoughts of what I wanted him to do to me. Henny plus horny equals' naked bodies between the sheets just'a bumpin' and a grindin'. I don't want our relationship to start out with sex. Thankfully the song ended and I was able to regroup and get back to thinking clearly.

"Wanda? Are you there?"

At first my voice came out with sounds of lust. I cleared my throat, closed my legs and sat upright in the bed.

"Yes, Braxton, I'm here." I should have said more.

"You don't have to say anything. Just know that I find you very attractive. You're smart, funny and caring. Yeah, my feet may be one of my imperfections but that, just like everything else, can be fixed. I want to get to know you – with all of your imperfections. Give me a chance...I'm the best man for you."

There was and is no reason that I shouldn't give Braxton a try. I've dated all types of men but never had a man that just put it in my face like that. I'm the one for you. I really want to find out why he's the one for me. No desperation...still I hope that he is.

"Hey, Pretty Lady, I'll give you a few pennies for your thoughts if you have dinner with me tomorrow night. We can talk about whatever you want. I'll tell you everything you need to know about me. I'm an open book for you. Reading me will be your pleasure."

"And what a pleasure it will be. I'm looking forward to tomorrow. Good night, Braxton."

"Good night, Pretty Lady."

159

And just like that my life began anew. A closed mind is a long trail to nowhere. I believe Braxton is my good thing. Yeah, he needs a couple 24 hour pedicures, but that's a small thing in a lifetime full of promise. Hmmmmm, will I be able to proclaim that Braxton is dating Wanda? Sometimes you gotta get out of your own way. Luther is singing, For You To Love and as I always say, everybody needs a little luv.

∞ *About the Author* ∞

Dating Wanda is the third book from Wanda D. Hudson. Wait for Love: A Black Girl's Story is the first. A collection of romantic short stories titled, LuvMe followed shortly after. Miss Hudson has a story included in the NY Times Bestselling Zane anthology, Succulent - Chocolate Flava ll, and a story in the Zane anthology, Purple Panties.

Wanda D, Hudson is also the fabulous standup comedian known as Miss WandaLuv. She's also a local radio personality in the Albany NY area.

Please visit Wanda D. Hudson's website – www.wandadhudson.com - to read excerpts and to stay in the know about this sexy dynamic writer.

Wanda D. Hudson

®Miss Luv's Books

Because Everybody Needs A Little Luv!